W9-BNG-102

COMING OUT
aLex

sylvia aguilar-zéleny

EPIC
Press

Alex
Coming Out: Book #6

Written by Sylvia Aguilar-Zéleny

Copyright © 2016 by Abdo Consulting Group, Inc.

Published by EPIC Press™
PO Box 398166
Minneapolis, MN 55439

Cover design by Nicole Ramsay
Images for cover art obtained from Shutterstock.com
Edited by Nancy Cortelyou

LIBRARY OF CONGRESS CATALOGING-IN-PUBLICATION DATA

Aguilar-Zéleny, Sylvia.
Alex / Sylvia Aguilar-Zéleny.
p. cm. — (Coming out)
Summary: Alex is a girl who believes she was born in the wrong body. So when
she finally shares the truth about herself to her best friend, Alex discovers how
challenging life can be for a small town transsexual.
ISBN 978-1-68076-008-8 (hardcover)
1. Transsexuals—Fiction. 2. Coming out (Sexual orientation)—Fiction. 3. Young
adult fiction. I. Title.
[Fic]—dc23
2015932730

EPIC
Press

EPICPRESS.COM

In memory of Leelah Alcorn, and everyone who has ever been forced deny their true spirit

CHAPTER ONE
DiCK OR DYKE

MY NAME IS ALEXANDRA. I DON'T LIKE IT. I ACTUALLY hate it. It's too long, it's too boring, it's too girly, and it's so not me. When I was six, I asked everyone to call me Alex. It's short, it's catchy, and it's not girly. It's way more like me.

Dad calls me Alexandra when he's mad, and/or he's trying to remind me (and everyone else) that I am a girl. His girl. I keep telling him, "Call me Alex, Dad." Seriously, how difficult is that? He says he can call me whatever the fuck he wants. I wanna say, "You call me whatever the fuck I want," but cursing would only make things worse, because he doesn't like me doing it. Fucking unbelievable. I grew up hearing fucks, shits, and motherfuckers from the men of my family and learned to use these words when needed, because when you live on a farm you need the cursing, believe me.

I live in London. No, not that one. I live in London, Ohio. We have a farm. I live with my father and my brother, Joe. My brother, Elliot, joined the Army and is now at a base in San Antonio, Texas. My mom died when I was born, so it's always been just the four of us. People sometimes ask me if I miss her, but you don't really miss what you never had. To me, *Mom* is just a word. *Mom* is the woman whose pictures are all over our walls.

My dad was also in the Army, but he got hurt. He's now a disabled vet turned farmer; we have horses, chickens, and two cows. The chickens and cows are just for us—strawberries are our business. Dad started growing them after Mom died. Everyone knows strawberries were her favorite fruit. When I was little I used to think strawberries were like hearts. So as we grew strawberries, we grew hearts. Hearts for Mom.

Dad always says that once Joe decides what to do with his life and I am off to college, he'll sell it all. He says he is sick and tired of the farm. We don't believe him. For starters, he loves this place as much as he complains about it; secondly, what would he do? I cannot picture him without seeing him riding his horse around our fields, yelling at everyone and everything. If anything, he should just retire and leave the farm to me.

"My name is Alex and I wanna be a farmer," I say in first period geometry. It's the beginning of the school year and we all have to introduce ourselves and tell the class something unique about us even though we've known each other since forever. Everybody laughs, of course, but I don't give a damn.

Stupid Philip Carson says, "Oh, for God's sake,

you should just get married and have kids. Don't you know farms are for men?"

Maggie stands up for me. She says, "What would you know? You're like half a man." It is my turn to laugh.

Our teacher, Mrs. Lee, tries to calm things down, but Philip says, "Oh, forgive me, Maggie, I forget your friend here is hardly a girl." Then he looks at me and says, "Listen everybody, this is Alex and she'll be the first dyke farmer in town."

I can't stand it. I hate that word. I stand up and punch fucking Philip Carson in the face so hard he falls off his chair. His nose bleeds. He wants to punch me back, but Mrs. Lee and some other kids stop him. He yells, "You see how she punches, she punches like a dyke, 'cause she's *a dyke!*"

I wanna fucking punch him again. In every single school in this country there's always an asshole-dickhead. In our school the title goes to Philip fucking Carson.

* * *

We're outside the vice principal's office now. Philip is giving me the eye from his chair, saying nothing, he got us here after all. They're gonna call Dad and he'll be so pissed off.

"Jenkins, come on in," Mr. Harris, the vice principal calls me. Philip stands up, but Mr. Harris tells him to wait for his turn. Mr. Harris closes the door behind me and asks me to sit down. Before saying anything, he calls Dad. "Mr. Jenkins? Hi, Mr. Harris here. I'm calling you in regards your daughter, Alex. Today in class, she and this other kid . . ."

Kid, he says. He doesn't say *boy*, he doesn't say *Philip*. *Kid*, he says. Like that will make things even.

Mr. Harris then explains the whole thing to my dad. I bet he's mad. I wonder what the punishment will be. Then Mr. Harris hands me the phone and says, "Your father wants to talk to you."

I frown, and as soon as I say, "Hey, Dad," Dad storms, "You promised me to be better this year. You promised me no more fights, Alexandra. I'll tell you if you continue on this way, you can say goodbye to college, you can say goodbye to—"

I interrupt him and state, "I don't care. I don't even wanna go to college. You know that. And stop calling me Alexan—" Dad hangs up on me.

I return the phone to Mr. Harris. He hangs up the phone, stares at me, and lets out a big breath before saying, "Look, Alexandra . . . "

I say, "Alex, please."

Mr. Harris nods.

"Look, Alex, I'm afraid you just got yourself three days of detention."

I can't help but bark, "But Philip started the whole thing! He should get detention, not me!"

"Oh, believe me, he's in trouble too. Now, go

with Miss Newton. She will give you the details of your detention."

"But . . . "

"But nothing, Alex. You argue, you get five days instead of three."

"Fine."

As I start to stand up, Mr. Harris says, "Send Philip in. Oh, and please go apologize to Mrs. Lee. It seems you keep making her classroom your own boxing ring. Now, head back to class and stay out of trouble."

"Okay."

As I walk out, he stops me and asks, "Alex, can I ask you a question?" I nod, and then he goes, "You really don't want to go to college? Or is that something you just said?"

I frown and tell him, "I dunno."

But I do know. I don't wanna go to college. I just wanna be on our farm. My brother Joe doesn't understand why I wanna be in charge of it. "It's simple," I tell him. "The farm is the only place I can be me."

He says, "You're bonkers, you know that?"

Joe hates the farm. All he likes are cars and motorcycles. He wants to race in Indiana. He's got an old Chevy that he's been working on for years. That Chevy is his love, his baby, and his life.

Joe finished high school almost two years ago and has no plans for his future. He used to work with my dad on the farm, but now he has a part-time job at Stanley Manufacturing, working on cars, of course. Dad didn't like the idea of him working there, but I guess it's better than having Joe bitching all the time.

Joe taught me how to fight when we were in middle school. He got tired of getting into fights for whatever his little sister did. I can't help it. You bully me and I'm all fists and kicks.

Joe and Dad think that one of these days my big mouth will get me in deep shit. There's nothing they can do about it. This is who I am. I know I'm screwed when Dad's first sentence is, "What am I going to do with you, Alexandra?" He looks at me like he wants to kill me with his bare hands. "Why can't you be normal? Why aren't you just a normal girl?" he adds.

I wanna tell him, "Because I ain't a normal girl, because I don't even wanna be a girl," but I keep my mouth shut. He wouldn't understand. How can I explain it? I am a girl, yes, but I have never felt like one.

I was born in the wrong body.

* * *

Jake meets me in the hall and asks if it's true that I punched Philip Carson. I tell him, "Yeah, I fucking did."

He laughs and says, "You did? I thought Maggie was just messing around."

"Maggie? You talked to her?" I ask him.

"Kind of," Jake opens his locker and grabs his

stuff. "Come on, let's go home. I'll tell you all about it."

Jake is my best friend. We were six when we met. His family moved to London after Jake's grandfather passed away. They inherited his farm, which is right across from ours. My dad was the one who told me our new neighbors had a kid my age.

I went to Jake's farm the very next day. I was excited. No kids my age lived around our farm. And my brothers, well, they were older, so they hated my being around them.

Jake was outside his house, playing cars. "I like your ride," I said when I saw his red Hot Wheels. I sat down next to him. "Who are you?" he asked.

"I'm Alex, I live on that farm." I had my big yellow Tonka Truck with me, my favorite toy those days.

Jake looked at it with fascination, and "Wanna trade rides?" And so we did. We spent that afternoon building roads and bridges.

Jake's mom came out and found us playing.

"Jake, it's time for dinner, hey . . . who's your friend?"

"This is Alex, Mom. We're playing, see?"

I explained to her that I lived across the road. "My dad is Ralph Jenkins," I said.

"Oh, you're Ralph's kid?" she said. She was looking at me as if trying to recognize my dad's features in my face. Instead, she saw my mom's. "You have your mother's eyes, no doubt."

I was surprised. I looked at her and said, "Everybody says I have Dad's face."

"I guess you do," she said, "but your eyes—those are your Mom's."

"Did you know my mom?"

"I did. We were friends when we were kids . . . Oh, this was ages ago. It's such a shame what happened to her. It must be hard to . . . Oh, what am I saying? What did you say your name is?"

"Alex."

"Well, *Alex*, I'm Debbie. Nice to meet you. Jake, should we invite Alex for dinner?"

"Oh, yes, yes, let's. Alex, can you stay for dinner?"

"Well, I guess he has to ask his dad first—right, Alex?"

I don't know why, but I didn't correct him.

The three of us walked over to my place. Luckily Dad was parking our truck.

"Hey, Ralph."

"Debbie, how are you? Have you guys finished moving in?"

"I don't think we ever will. It's a never-ending job."

Then, Dad looked at Jake and me and said, "I see these two have met."

"Yes, they have. The boys have been playing together all afternoon. We actually invited him over for dinner. Is that okay with you?"

My dad was like, "*boys?*" His eyes went from me, to Jake, and back to me. That was probably the moment when Dad realized his little girl was more like a little boy. "Alexandra is my *daughter*, Debbie. She is a girl," Dad said.

It was as if he had broken a spell.

Jake and his mom looked at me. I felt like I'd just been turned into an ugly frog. Jake asked, "You're a girl?" I didn't know what to say.

Jake's mom didn't know what to say either, "No, no, I should have noticed. I just . . . his clothes, I mean, *her* clothes . . . I thought . . . of course, of course Alex is a girl. Look at her," she said, trying to find the girl hiding in me.

I decided to interrupt and go back to what really mattered to me, "So, can I have dinner at Jake's or not?"

My dad smiled, and said, "Of course you can. Here, take these for dessert," and Dad got a small basket of strawberries from the truck.

"Thank you, and again, I'm sorry. I am such an idiot . . . "

My dad sighed. "It happens all the time. This one here could sure use a feminine touch," he said, laughing.

* * *

As we were walking back to Jake's home, his mom continued apologizing. "How could I not see it?" she said.

"Well, maybe because *she* looks like a *he*," Jake replied.

"Jake, sweetie, that's not a nice thing to say," Jake's mom said. "Alex is your friend. Apologize to her."

Jake looked at me and said, "Sorry, Alex."

I shrugged.

Debbie looked at me. "So your name is Alexandra?"

I nodded.

"So what do you want us to call you, Alexandra or Alex?"

I smiled and said, "Alex, please."

Debbie smiled, and as we arrived to their house,

she said, "Alex it is. Now you two go wash your hands."

I followed Jake to the bathroom. When he turned on the light, I saw myself in the mirror. I saw a kid. I didn't see a boy or a girl, just a kid. I didn't understand what the big deal was.

Jake asked, "Why didn't you tell me you were a girl?"

I shrugged. "I don't know."

"Why do you play with cars and stuff?"

"Because dolls just stand there and do nothing." I stood still, pretending to be a doll; I even faked a pose and happy face. Then added, "Plus, cars are way more fun, duh!"

Jake said, "You're right! Dolls are just like this," and he also faked being a doll.

When it was time for me to go home, Jake walked me back. I invited him to see our foal.

"You have one?" he asked.

"Yes, and it is beautiful." I took him to our barn.

"Wow, it really is beautiful. Is it a she or a he?"

"Oh, I never asked," I said, and we both laughed.

I gave Jake a tour through our barn. He asked me if I was allowed to play there. "Yup," I said. "I play here all the time."

"Can we play here tomorrow?"

"Sure," I said.

We've been friends ever since. We would play at his place or mine. Jake and I sometimes fought over stupid stuff, but we always found a way to fix things. He's like a brother that I actually like. Jake gets me. He's never seen me as the girl next door. To him I'm just Alex, his best friend.

* * *

As we are leaving school, Jake asks me what happened at the principal's office. "What did they tell you?"

"Same shit," I say. "Starting tomorrow I get detention, but only for three days."

"Till next time?"

I give him the finger.

"And that's why, ladies and gentlemen, everyone calls Alex the D word," he says, laughing.

We pass Philip Carson on our way.

"Don't you open your poisoned mouth," I say.

Philip ignores me and continues talking to his friends. Everyone looks at us outside school. It seems the news had already spread: *Alex punched Philip.*

"Alex, man, you gotta chill out. Hey, where are our . . . ?" Jake looks everywhere in the parking lot.

"No bikes today, remember? We walked."

"Fuck, and with this weather."

Jake and I normally ride our bikes to school, but his is broken and he wouldn't ride with me on mine. He doesn't trust my riding skills. It's not that far from school to home, but it's hot. Really hot.

"We need to learn how to drive," Jake declares. "Maybe your brother would teach us?"

"Yeah, right," I reply. "Joe will never let us close to his *baby.*"

"Dude, he's got a thing with that car. I'm sure he makes out with it every night."

"I bet he does."

"Has he bought that new engine?"

"I don't know. He's still not talking to me."

"Really?"

"Yup."

"But it wasn't your fault!" Jake yells. "He bailed on you at the fair."

"And I tried to cover for him, but my old man is too smart for that."

"So, where did Joe go anyway?"

"No clue. He was gone most of this weekend too."

"Maybe your brother has a double life," Jake says, laughing.

"It's either that or he has a secret girlfriend."

* * *

Dad had stuff to do the morning of the fair in Springfield, so he sent Joe and me to set up the stall and start selling our strawberries. Joe helped me with the setting up, but then he left. He just left. Not a word.

When Dad arrived, Joe wasn't back yet. "Are you on your own? Where's your brother?"

"I dunno. Hey, can I go buy a corn dog?" I said, trying to avoid his question. He answered with another question.

"What time did he go?"

"Please, can I go buy a corn dog? I'm starving." I was just trying to change the subject.

"Okay, but first call your brother, I want him here ASAP." Dad handed me his cell phone.

I called Joe and told him to come back because Dad was asking for him, but my dad took the phone and started yelling, "I asked you to be in charge of the stall. Where are you? Get back here now."

I said, "I took care of everything . . . "

But Dad ignored me.

Dad wants to rely on Joe for everything instead of me. He doesn't think I'm fit for the job even though I've been doing the same shit as my brothers since I was a kid. And the only reason he doesn't trust me to do it is because I'm a girl. He thinks that the *girl of the house* should clean the shit in the barn and not be in charge of anything else.

As we get home, I ask Jake to tell me about Maggie.

"There's nothing to say," he replies.

"But you talked to her, didn't you?"

"Not really, she just said 'Hey,' and I said, 'Hey, yourself,' and then she told me about you and Philip."

"What exactly did she tell you?"

"Well . . . she said that you punched Carson in class, and that I should teach you how to control your animal instincts."

"She said that?"

"No."

"Do you still love her?" Jake ignores me. "Do you? Do you still love her?"

"Shut up, Alex."

"I'm just trying to help, here," I say. "Don't give me attitude." But he's already off to his house.

"I love you, Jake!" I yell.

He gives me the finger and yells back, "You are a dick, Alex!" He pauses, and then says, "Hey, come help me fix my bike later?"

"Only if you tell me if you love me."

"I fucking love you, Alex, even when you're a dick."

"Better a dick than a dyke," I respond.

* * *

Maggie. I met her before Jake did, back when we were still kids. We were seven or so. It was the summer that Jake went to visit his cousins in Akron. I was bored to death. Dad told me he was going to help an old friend with his barn in West Jefferson, only a few miles from here, and invited me to come along.

"He's got a kid almost your age. You can play."

I took my yellow truck, some of my Legos, and jumped into my dad's pickup, all happy. When we arrived, I looked for the *kid almost my age* everywhere.

The guy greeted my dad. "Oh, is this Alex?" he asked as he noticed me.

"Yes, she's looking forward to playing with Maggie," Dad explained.

"Maggie, come over here and meet Alex."

Maggie was beautiful, like a doll; she was wearing a flowery dress and a pair of purple Crocs with a pink bow on the front. But Maggie wasn't a doll—a boring, stiff doll. Maggie was real.

"This is Alex. She came to play with you."

Maggie looked at me. Her eyes inspected my tennis shoes, my shorts, my sleeveless shirt, and my Cincinnati Bengals cap.

"She?" Maggie asked her dad while looking at me. "*She* looks like a boy."

"Maggie, don't be rude!" her dad said.

"Don't worry," Dad said, "it happens all the

time. I guess it's my fault. I buy her clothes and I know nothing 'bout girl stuff."

Maggie looked at me again and asked me in a low voice, "Are you a girl? You don't look like a girl."

A big lump stuck in my throat. I felt like crying. I felt like running away. I felt stupid. I nodded *yes* with my head.

"Show Alex your room. You two can play in there. We've got work to do outside."

Maggie's room looked like those rooms you see in a Target furniture catalog. Pink and perfectly girly. She had dolls and Barbies and babies and coloring books with flowers and ladybugs.

"What'd you have in there?" Maggie asked pointing at my backpack.

"My toys."

"Let's see."

I pulled out my yellow truck, a few cars, and my Legos.

"Are those *yours*?" Maggie asked.

"Yes, why? What's wrong?" I asked, but I already

knew what was wrong with them. My toys were for boys, and girls like her did not play with toys for boys. I had learned that in school from the girls in my class who kept mocking me for playing with cars or role-playing Transformers with Jake on the playground.

"Nothing, I'm just asking. Do you have dolls too?" Maggie said checking out my backpack.

"Not here."

"Well, then let's play with mine." She started showing me her shelf of dolls. It was like a display in the girls' section of Toys"R"Us.

"Pick one," she said.

"I have a better idea," I said, "You play with your Barbies, and my truck can be your ride," I said, setting up my big truck on her carpet. "We can imagine this is the Farmers' parade. And, with these," I pointed at my Legos. "I can even build you whatever you want."

She looked at my toys, and then looked at me again.

"Oh, yes, yes. We can also build a house. Here, I have these." Maggie opened the door to a big tower of shoeboxes.

"Cool," I said.

We designed a whole furniture set for Maggie's doll house. It took us like an hour before we actually got to play. When we were done she said, "Oh, wait, I know! If you like boy stuff, you're gonna love this." Maggie climbed the highest shelf in her room and got Barbie's Ken. "You can play with this. You can be my boyfriend."

I looked at her, understanding and not understanding. I agreed. I became Maggie's boyfriend. I liked it.

After a while we got hungry and went to get a snack.

Her mom was in the kitchen. "Are you guys having fun?" she asked.

"Yeah. I'm Barbie and Alex is Ken. We're sweethearts. She's my boyfriend."

Her mom laughed, and asked, "Your boyfriend?"

"Yes, my *Barbie's* boyfriend."

"Oh, well Maggie, make sure you girls change turns so Alex gets to be Barbie too."

Maggie disappointedly said, "Oh, but I want Alex to be Ken. I like her being my boyfriend." And she held my hand. Our fingers intertwined.

Maggie's mom gave me this weird look. The same everyone still gives me when finding out I'm not a boy, but a girl. She didn't say anything else, though, and fixed some tuna sandwiches for us.

When we finished, she asked us to bring lemonade to our fathers. "And help them. Maybe they can finish already."

We "helped" our dads with the barn for a while until I needed to go to the bathroom. Maggie told me where it was and I went on my own inside her house. Maggie's mom was talking on the phone, she was telling someone that Ralph and his daughter were here. She said, "You were absolutely right. This family needs a woman. Alex is a little weird. Maggie wants her to be her *boyfriend.* Her

30

Barbie's boyfriend. That's normal, but it was like Maggie wanted Alex to be *her* boyfriend. And Alex, oh my God, she seemed happy about it. She is so *different*."

Sometimes you don't understand something, but at the same time you do because it hurts. Some words land on your skin and bruise. I was bruised. I ended up crying in the bathroom. Then, I cleaned up and ran to the barn.

"I wanna go now," I told Dad.

"Wait, Alex, let me finish my lemonade."

"I wanna go NOW," I cried.

"Are you okay?" Maggie looked at me, as if trying to understand what had changed.

"Girls," Maggie's dad sighed. "Who understands them?"

"Not me, for sure," Dad replied.

* * *

Once in the car, Dad started asking me random questions:

"Did you get all your stuff?"

"Yes."

"Did you have fun?"

"More or less."

"Are you hungry?"

"No."

"Alex, what is it? I thought you were having fun. You and Maggie seemed like you were getting along."

"But her mother thinks I'm weird. She says I'm *different*."

"Alex, I don't understand you."

"Yes, you do. You always say the same thing."

"Look, Alex, I . . . "

"This is your fault."

"My fault?"

"It's your fault. It's all your fault! Look at me."

I wasn't blaming Dad for bringing me along. I

wasn't blaming him for buying me boy clothes. I was blaming Dad because I wasn't a boy.

As soon as we got home I ran to my room and locked myself in. I cried and cried and cried.

That was the day I learned once and for all that I was different.

A few years later Maggie started school here in London. London is a small town and she ended up in the same school that Jake and I went to. She and I would smile at each other from time to time, but we weren't friends.

We started talking at some point in our last year of middle school because Jake had a big crush on her. We all became friends. We spent a whole summer together; the three of us—here, there, everywhere. She even got a bike and started riding to the lake with us.

At one point Maggie decided we should do stuff, just us girls. We did. We would hang out and bike around town. Once she insisted on doing a makeover on me. She invited me over to her house.

"But your mom hates me," I told her.

"She doesn't, besides it's her book club day. My dad is out of town. Come on, say yes. It'll be just the two of us."

"Fine."

She plucked my eyebrows, waxed my mustache. She gave me a face massage, which was the best of all. It was nice to feel her hands all over. She colored my eyes, my lips, did my hair, and she made me wear some of her clothes. I became her real life doll.

Then it all turned weird.

We sorta kissed. But I didn't start it, she did. She asked me if I had ever kissed someone. I said, "No, never have, and never will."

She said, "Don't say that. You never know when you'll meet *the one*."

She insisted that all girls needed to know how to kiss. "I'll teach you," she said. "It's easy." I was sitting on her bed and she kneeled down in front of me. She pulled me by the shoulders so I could be closer to her. "Ready?" she asked.

"Not really," I said. She slid her hands down my shoulders to my wrists. She held me by the hands. Then she said, "Just close your eyes."

And we kissed. I expected a short, quick kiss. Instead, her lips caressed mine, and her tongue found a way inside my mouth. That's when I jumped back. "Stop," I said.

Maggie looked away and said, "Relax, it's okay— we're friends. I won't tell anyone." I picked up my stuff, took a tissue from her nightstand, cleaned my face and left.

I never hung out with her again without Jake. We never talked about it. I never told Jake about it. It was like it never happened.

But it did.

And no matter how much I tried to forget the whole thing, I couldn't. Maggie's kiss would visit my dreams once in a while.

Jake and Maggie were together for a while and just before we started our sophomore year of high school, they broke up. It caught me by surprise. It seemed like everything was going well between them. He didn't wanna talk about it. So, I did what buddies do for each other. I let him be.

I know it sounds horrible, but I was actually happy to have Jake just to myself again.

CHAPTER TWO
Lady of the house

MY DAD'S MAD AT ME. I SCREWED UP AGAIN WITH stupid Philip Carson. "It's just been a month, Alexandra," he says. I try to explain to him that it wasn't entirely my fault, but he won't listen.

I yell, "He called me a DYKE! I'm supposed to do nothing about it?"

Dad looks at me and says, "Dyke? Why would he call you that?," but he knows perfectly why. Story of my life. He then adds, "You're gonna get yourself hurt one of these days, girl. Now, set the table. Dinner's ready."

We sit down and start eating in silence. Joe arrives a little bit later. He is not talking to either of us. We are almost growling at each other. Dad is mad at me. Dad is mad at Joe. Joe is mad at me. Damn. Finally, Dad breaks the silence, "Alex punched a kid at school."

"Again?" my brother asks. "Who?"

"Philip Carson," I reply.

"Henry's brother again?" Joe asks.

"Yeah."

Dad says, "Tell him why, Alexandra."

"He called me a dyke."

My brother closes his eyes and says *no* with his head, then goes, "He's an asshole, just like Henry. Did I ever tell you guys I kicked Henry in the balls once?"

"Ha ha, you did? Why?" I ask.

"I don't even remember," my brother says. "But I'm sure I had a good reason."

Dad adds, "Didn't Elliot kick the other brother's ass, too?"

"Ken?" I ask.

"Yes, he did," Joe answers with a grin. "It was because of a girl."

"Those Carson kids are dicks, just like their father," Dad muses. "Although, they probably think the same of us," Dad states.

I look at him and ask, "Have you ever punched Mr. Carson?"

"No, but believe me, I've had reasons to," Dad says smiling.

We all end up laughing. Joe and I take turns describing our fights with the Carson kids. Dad tells us about the time Elliot fought with the eldest brother. I finally say, "I miss Elliot."

Joe smiles, and Dad responds, "We all do."

We finish eating, and as Joe and I pick up the plates, Dad makes himself some coffee. I'm washing the dishes and Dad shakes my shoulders while saying, "You have to be more careful, Alex. One of these days you're really going to get in trouble."

I like it when he calls me Alex, just like Joe and Elliot do.

* * *

Elliot is eight years older than me. He always said he was going to join the Army or the Air Force. My dad didn't like the idea, so he made Elliot promise to get a degree first, any degree, at the community college. Then, and only then, could Elliot do whatever the hell he wanted.

Elliot went to Columbus State Community College, which is about forty minutes from the farm. He would come and go almost every day for two years or so. During that time, Dad did his best to convince him to transfer his credits to a university, but Elliot refused and went off to the Army.

It's been almost two years since he left. We were all sad to see him go. If my family were a sandwich, Elliot would be the mayonnaise: he was what stuck us all together. He was Dad's right hand when it came to the house. He and Joe were more like best friends than brothers. Elliot always found time for me, too—to play with me, watch TV with me, take care of me.

Elliot acted like the *lady of the house* or something like that. He was in charge of the grocery shopping, making dinner, etc. Dad also cooks—he makes the best meatloaf in the world—but before leaving, it was Elliot who was in charge of feeding the troops.

Elliot was also in charge of me. He made sure I ate, showered, brushed my teeth, did my homework, and stayed out of trouble. I bet everything was a piece of cake, except for the last part.

Before leaving, Elliot told me it was my turn to be *lady of the house*. I was like, "No way."

He smiled. "Joe can't even cook an egg, and Dad—well, he does cook, but he works all day. Wouldn't it be nice for him to arrive home to dinner already made?" He had made his point. But, believe me, I am far from being the *lady of the house*.

I especially liked Elliot telling me stories about

Dad being in the Army or stories about Mom. To this day, the image I have of my mother comes from Elliot's stories. Dad doesn't talk about her all that much. It's like it still hurts him to mention her name. Joe thinks Dad should go out more and start dating. I feel the same. Dad says that he is off the market.

When Elliot left, I took his room. I didn't change a thing in it. I still have the *Taxi Driver* poster on the door, although I have never even watched the movie. The egg cartons are still tacked to the walls, which is great because I can have the music up as loud as I want and Dad doesn't yell at me, at least not as much as he did when I was in my old room.

I moved because my room never felt like my room. It was the room my mom designed for me while she was pregnant. It's cotton-candy pink with some drawings in lavender and purple. I never dared to change the color because she drew it all. My walls are a parade of animals and flowers and butterflies and little houses with little people. Dad would have killed me if I had done anything to cover all that shit up. Mom's work.

After dinner, Dad asks Joe and me to clean up the kitchen. He asks me if I have homework.

"Just a short composition," I tell him.

Dad makes himself some coffee and goes out to the porch to drink it. Once I hear the slam on the front door, I tell Joe, "How about I do my homework in like a second and then we watch an episode of *The Walking*—"

"No zombies for me today, Alex. I'm going out."

"Where to?"

"None of your business."

"Come on, Joe. It's the one thing we do together."

"Sorry, kiddo. Got plans," he said, and he left.

Elliot would have never, ever said no to a night of *The Walking Dead*. Never.

I grab my backpack and start my homework.

* * *

Dad threatens to sell the farm every once in a while—like when he sees any critter around our crops, or when a deal doesn't happen the way he wants it to.

Joe always replies, "Well, do it, just sell the damn place already." I tell him I would die like a dry strawberry if he did. I can't imagine my life without being on the farm. This is my home. This is my past, my present, and my future.

Jake says I'm the only one who actually cares about the family farm.

Elliot joined the Army for the same reason my dad did, to escape from the farm. And Joe, who knows what he wants? Besides his car and working at Stanley Manufacturing? He does like fixing things around here, but when it comes to the actual work, he's nowhere to be found. Joe is a bit weird. He's a bit distant from our family. Not to his friends, though; he's texting or talking on his phone all the freaking time.

No matter how much my dad tries to get him

involved in the farm, Joe's not up for it. What I would do to have Joe's chances, to have his body. To have my dad's support.

The Walking Dead is on. I decide to finish my composition later and lie down on the sofa. I fucking love this show. My favorite character used to be Daryl because he's brave, he's a loner, and he does whatever the fuck he wants. I wish he wasn't having that thing with Carol. Not that I'm jealous, not at all. It's just, he should always be a loner. He's the man I wish I could be.

You may think that I became this sort of tomboy because I was surrounded by men. That might be a reason, but the way I see it, I had a choice, and I chose what I wanted.

I have this memory of turning six or seven years old and being in a big store in Columbus.

Dad's telling me, "Choose a toy, anything you want."

"Anything I want? Really?"

"Yes."

He had just made a big sale in Columbus so he was in a spending mood.

I walked through all the aisles of the toy section trying to find what I wanted. I stood for a while in the Barbies and dolls section. I liked them okay, but mostly I liked looking at them right where they were. They didn't call my attention for anything else, not for playing anyways.

Dad decided to give me some time. "Look, I'm gonna get some stuff for your brothers. I'll be back."

I looked and looked, but nothing caught my attention. For a second, I even considered getting a Mulan doll. She was like my favorite character ever and *Mulan II* had just been released. But then I saw *it*. Right there on a top shelf, yellow and bright, a big caterpillar truck, just like the one Joe had once, the one he'd destroyed in like a second. I grabbed it. It was huge and heavy and beautiful and it smelled like new plastic.

"This, I want this," I told Dad when he came back. He looked at me and then took a look at my

Tonka. He smiled. I guess he found it funny that I wanted a truck.

"Are you sure? What about that?" He pointed to the Mulan dolls. "Isn't that your favorite princess?" he said.

"Yes, but I don't want it," I said. "I want this truck. And Mulan isn't a princess, Dad. She is a warrior."

"Oh, well . . . How about a doll and the truck?"

I did like Mulan, so I said, "Deal." I never paid as much attention to Mulan as I did to my truck. She moved onto the same shelf where all my other dolls lived. Until they didn't, because once Jake and I became best friends, my dolls became our enemies.

Once Jake and I played a war in which our improvised weapons would kill each and every one of my dolls. The ones who survived the war ended up bald and naked with no feet because I had chewed their feet. I made weird beings out of them, beings that were neither girls nor boys.

Even though Dad knew I preferred trucks over dolls, he kept buying them for me. Dolls. I like to look at them. Just like sometimes I like looking at girls; they are pretty and they are something I am not. Do I like girls? I do and I don't. I can't get along all that well with them. Could I fall in love with a girl? I hope not, girls are all about gossip and looks and shit.

The show is over. I turn the TV off and finish my homework. I take a long shower and go to my room. I comb my hair. It's getting really long. I hate it. I have this blonde curly hair that makes me look so stupid. If I keep it short, it's just wavy. But if I let it grow a little longer, I become Goldilocks. That was my nickname in elementary school. Goldilocks and Jake the Bear, they used to call us, because at that time Jake was really chubby.

My hair is a mess. Maybe I should go get a haircut tomorrow. I start falling asleep before ten p.m., but then about midnight, I hear Joe coming in. He wakes Dad up too.

Dad yells, "Joe, that you?"

"Yup."

"It's late."

"Is it?"

Then silence. I close my eyes again. I wanna go back to my dream of me being Daryl and hunting zombies all over London, Ohio.

* * *

Today has been an uneventful day at school, except for Philip Carson trying to sweet talk Maggie and her friends at lunch, and Maggie sending him straight to hell. I sometimes miss her hanging out with us. Jake pretended to be so busy eating lunch, acting as if he didn't care. But I am sure he liked that Maggie gave Phillip a hard time.

So Philip goes and finds himself a new victim, he starts making fun of a kid I've never seen. He's tall, with pink hair. Pink. The kid says something to Philip—I can't tell what it is—and then stupid

Philip gives pink hair kid the finger and goes back to his pack of dogs.

"Did you see that?" I ask Jake.

"No, what?"

"Never mind."

"Hey, Alex, what you doing after dinner? I have this big assignment with Jerry, my chemistry partner. We're meeting at the coffeehouse. Wanna come?"

"No, I'm gonna get my hair cut."

"Come on, you can do that some other day. Please, I can't put up with Jerry on my own."

"Jerry's not that bad, just pretend his jokes are actually funny."

"Like I do with yours."

"Shut up."

"So, you're not coming."

"Nope. I told ya, I got plans."

* * *

I'm getting ready to go to Hortense's when the

phone rings. I answer and this sweet, sweet voice asks me if Joe is home.

"Yes, who's this?"

"Mia," she says.

"Mia?" I had never heard that name. Although, it's not like Joe tells us about his friends all that much.

I yell, "Joe, Mia's on the phone."

I hear Joe running down the stairs.

"Mia . . . who is she?" I ask.

Joe swoops in and grabs the phone and says what has become his classic line: "None of your business." Then he sweeps his hands through the air, motioning for me to disappear.

I walk into the living room. Dad is watching some documentary on World War II, his favorite subject. I ask him for money and tell him I'm going to bike downtown to Hortense's to get my hair cut.

He says, "Again? Your hair is fine. Actually, isn't it already too short?"

"No, Dad. It's too long. It's always in my face and I can't ride," I tell him. He glares at me while opening his wallet. I know he hates my hair short. Truth is, if it were up to me, I would shave it all off.

CHAPTER THREE
hair is Just hair

HORTENSE HAS ALWAYS CUT MY HAIR. I THINK SHE'S cut everyone's hair. Her mom did it before her, and before that, her grandmother was in charge. The women of her family probably cut the hair of the founders of the town. Hortense is like a hundred and two years old. She's the closest thing to a monument in London.

When I was a kid she never said a word about the way I dressed, but when I turned thirteen, she started nagging me about looking too boyish. "Wear more pink. Wear ribbons, flowers—something," she would say. Who wears ribbons and flowers at thirteen?

Sometimes she'd say, "You're so thin and tall. If I had your body I would always show it off in a dress instead of those old sweat pants that you wear all the time . . . " I got tired of explaining to her that I don't see myself as a lady, and that I find dresses stupid. I simply smile and say, "Oh, Hortense, if only I dared."

As I arrive at the hair salon I see that it's being painted. A woman I have never seen before is sweeping outside.

"Hi," I say. "Is Hortense in?"

"Hi," the woman responds. "Hortense is not . . . well, let's say I'm the new Hortense." She puts the broom to the side and invites me in.

"Whaddya mean you're the new Hortense?" I ask.

"Well," the woman says as she checks her own hair on the mirror, "I started working for Hortense last week, and I convinced her to make some changes to the place. It seems she's had it just the same since . . . "

"Like 1900, probably," I say.

The woman smiles and agrees with me. "You bet. Anyway, one thing led to another and I convinced her to lease me the place. My plan is to buy it from her."

"Wow," I say as I walk through the salon that has new stations and mirrors.

"I'm keeping the name, though. What'd you think?" The woman shows me a picture of what will be Hortense's new billboard, a vintage font in bright red.

"Yeah, this is like a historical place for everyone in town."

"And it looked like one, didn't it?" she adds.

I laugh. I like her right away. "My name is Alex. What's yours?"

"Nice to meet you, Alex. I'm Amanda."

Amanda is in her forties. She's a tall, redheaded woman with beautiful, dark-brown eyes. As I look at her, I notice she's looking at me too. She has started wondering if I am a girl or a boy, I know it. She checks me up and down from head to toe. Without saying a word, she takes my Cincinnati Bengals' cap off. She touches and pulls softly at my hair with her fingers while she looks at my face in the mirror.

"So, what are we going to do today, kiddo?" she asks. *Kiddo,* she is playing it safe.

"Just a trim here and here." I say as I point at sides and front of my hair.

"Okay. Let's wash you first." She walks me to the sink. I can picture her looking at me, still trying to figure me out. My boobs should give me away. They are small, but if I am in certain positions they pop out.

"So, Alex, what do you do for a living?" Amanda jokes.

"Oh, I'm a student," I answer. "I'm a sophomore at London High."

"Really? My son goes there. He's a sophomore, too. His name is George. George Flynn. Maybe you've met him?"

"George Flynn? Mmh . . . No," I say. "At least not yet. Classes just started."

"Oh, you're right. Well, you will. There's no way you can miss him. He's unique, with his short pink hair."

I remember him. He's the one who Philip tried to bully today. I refrain from mentioning anything about it to Amanda though. She finishes washing my hair and then pats my head with a towel.

"Well, if you see him bitching around or trying to ditch school, let me know. He hates living here."

"Bitching around?"

"Isn't that how y'all call it? As if there was nothing else to do in the world?" I shrug. I don't bitch around. I have too many things to do all the time.

As if I had asked Amanda to tell me her whole life story, she adds, "We used to live in Cincinnati, you know? And let's just say that I am trying to have a fresh start for the both of us. I'm a friend of one of Hortense's daughters and she did all the logistics for me. It's just fantastic how sometimes a friend can solve your whole life. Has that ever happened to you, Alex?" Amanda is done drying my hair with the towel and has now started to comb it.

"Not really," I say. "I don't have too many friends."

"I don't believe you. Everybody has at least one good friend."

"Well, yeah, I do have one."

"See? Tell me about your friend."

"His name is Jake. We've been friends since we were little. He's my neighbor, too, so we spent the summer biking, swimming . . . you know just hanging out."

Amanda is trimming my hair with the scissors, her hands move softly around my head. It feels nice.

"That sounds nice. What do you like most about Jake?"

"Well, I don't know. He's cool."

Amanda's hands are amazing. Hortense was okay, but Amanda's touch is soft. She runs her fingers over my scalp, and it feels so nice. She continues,

"But there must me something special that you like about him, right?"

My mind opens up like a photo album; each page is an episode of my life with Jake. Biking, hiking, playing ball, riding horses, making a mess in my dad's barn, cleaning up our messes in my dad's barn, wrestling, playing video games, smoking his dad's cigarettes in hiding, sneaking out at night to swim in the lake. I reply, "Jake's been my partner in crime since I can remember. We do everything together. He accepts me for who I am."

Wow, who said that last sentence? I have no idea where that came from. It seems my words also resonated in Amanda's mind because she stopped doing my hair for a second. She locks eyes with me in the mirror and says, "Isn't that beautiful? That's what friends are for. Oh, I wish George could find a friend like that. He needs someone to accept him for who he is. Someone besides me, that is."

I smile at Amanda, but don't know what to say.

"I obviously don't know how it's been for you,

but George had a horrible time as a teenager. He was always such an easygoing boy, and then all of a sudden he became something else. Bullying does that to people, you know? Because he was bullied *all the time*, until one day he struck back. Now he's always barking at everybody."

I understand what Amanda is saying; I bark too.

What is it about hairdressers? They make you open up, and then you don't know where to turn. I end up telling Amanda old stories about me and some of the kids at school. I tell her about all those times they made fun of me because I either looked like a boy or acted like one. I tell her about the time they locked me in a storage room when we were in elementary school.

Amanda listens to me, and even stops working on my hair for a while, sitting down in the chair next to me. At some point, she stands up and says, "Well, I should get back to my masterpiece. Alex, what exactly are you trying to do with your hair? I did trim it in the back, but I don't know what you are looking for in terms of style."

"I really don't care. You see, I always wear a cap or a beanie." Amanda looks at me and again I feel that she is trying to figure me out.

"If you only cover it, what's the point of having hair? Why don't we try something new? Tell me, why do you always wear a cap?"

"Well, because I hate it. I hate these curls." I pull out a strand of hair and show it to Amanda.

My hair has always been a mess. As a kid I never paid much attention to it. It sorta just grew. It was actually Hortense who taught me how to braid it and pull it in a ponytail so it wouldn't be in my face all the time. Then at around fourteen, I started cutting it shorter. I never let it go beyond my shoulders.

"Well, we can explore a bob cut, ear length. Very sexy, very French . . . " I must have made a face or something because before I could say anything Amanda continued, "But if we're looking for a more boyish look, we can just go ahead and keep it ultra-cropped with short bangs."

I like how Amanda says "we," as if *we* are in this together. I smile as Amanda shows me some pictures in a magazine, girls and boys with super short hair, then she says it. "You see, these models are androgynous, like you."

"They're what?" I ask.

Amanda then makes a face like she's made a mistake. She clears her throat and explains, "Androgynous. You know, people whose looks are part male and part female. People that . . . Oh my God, I didn't mean that. Alex, I'm sorry if I'm offending you in any way, I ..."

"No, no, no," I tell her and turn my chair around to look at her face to face. "I've just . . . I've never heard that word before."

Amanda blushes, and then laughs, and adds, "I have this thing . . . I feel like I can read people and since I saw you outside . . . Well, you just don't look like a girl who wants to look like a girl."

Amanda doesn't stumble over her words. She looks at me and I can see she means what she says.

I blush. I'm comfortable with her, yes, but what am I supposed to say? "Just tell me what *we* can do to my hair," I say.

Amanda smiles, goes over some of the images in the magazine, and points at a haircut. Short on the sides, a wisp of a bang. "We can try this. What'd you say? It will look good on you. Besides, hair is just hair. It always grows back."

Amanda is right. Hair is just hair. "Well, let's do it," I say.

Amanda gets an electric razor and goes over my sides. I ask her more about her life.

"So, you lived in Cincy before moving here?"

"Yes."

"I love Cincy. It's a great city. We don't go all that often but it's totally awesome."

"Yes, that's what George says. He says I couldn't have found a smaller town to live in. I guess he's right, but London has its own beauty."

"I guess."

We continue talking as if we had known each other forever. She goes on, "I mean, I understand this is different from the city, but why do kids have to question their parents all the time? Do you do that, Alex?"

"No," I say, and then change my mind. "Well, sometimes when my dad says he's going to sell our farm I tell him he is crazy."

"You guys have a farm?"

"Yes, Alice Strawberries—that's us. We also have cows and horses but our deal is strawberries. Ours are the best in the area."

"So, you like your farm?"

"Uh huh, a lot. But no one in my family does as much."

"Who else lives on this farm with you?"

"My dad and my two brothers—actually, just one of my brothers right now. The other one joined the Army." When I say I live with my dad and my brothers people always ask about my mom. But not Amanda. She says nothing.

"That's a lot of men in one house."

I smile.

"We're almost done. Let's rinse you off and dry your hair."

I look at myself in the mirror and my hair is just a mess—a clean mess, though. Amanda plays with my hair and says, "Wait. Once I dry it you will notice the difference."

I sit down and Amanda pulls my head to the bowl. She does not dampen my hair right away, but then I feel the warm water and Amanda's massaging my scalp. It feels nice.

We go back to the chair in front of the mirror. Amanda dries my hair with her fingers and explains to me how easy it will be for me to do it at home. She pours some product into her hand and moves her fingers here and there. I see myself.

"Is that a smile I see? You like it, Alex?"

"Yes, I definitely do. Thank you so much."

I try to pay her, but Amanda says, "First, give me a hug. You are my first client and my first favorite person in this town." I hug her. She pulls me closer and says, "Hope to see you again." I wave goodbye to Amanda.

I think Amanda is now my new favorite person in town. I get on my bike and feel my head. It's light. My hair is fresh. My hair is new. It's like a new me has just landed in my body.

As I arrive home, I see Jake outside taking his bike apart.

"What happened?" I ask him.

"It's broken, again. I had to cancel with Jerry." Then Jake looks up at me and seems surprised about my hair.

"Whoa, that's like super-short." He comes close to me and reaches for my hair, but I move backwards so he won't touch it.

"Hair is just hair," I tell him.

Jake looks at me, as if studying the whole of me. "You look . . . cute. It's like your eyes popped out."

"Cute? Me? Shut up." I'm embarrassed and change the subject. "Let me get my tools." As I walk home, I touch my hair. I don't feel cute—I feel cool, I feel different . . . Actually, I don't feel different. I feel more like myself.

Dad's in the exact same spot in the living room, watching TV. First, he looks at me without looking. Then, when he realizes there's something new about me, he stares at my hair. I can read his thoughts, *What did you do? Why?* But he says nothing.

I continue my way to my room and only as I start climbing the stairs, he says, "Too short. Way too short."

CHAPTER FOUR
happy birthday

TODAY IS SEPTEMBER TWENTY-FIRST. IT'S A FAMILY day, an even more important celebration than Thanksgiving or Christmas. It's my mom's birthday. Like every year, we'll go to the cemetery to place some fresh flowers, clean her plot, and hang out for a bit. It would be different if this was a day to talk about her, to get to know more about her, but Dad always prefers silence when it comes to Mom.

I've always tried to ask questions about Mom while visiting her grave. But not once have I ever gotten any answers. Only occasionally Dad says things like, "Not now," or "Some other time." Really? If not then, while we're right in front of her, when? Mom's like a secret that Dad hides. There's really nothing mysterious about her life or her death, but Dad has always dealt with the whole thing as if our mom was this suspense novel character that no one can unveil.

"Shotgun," I yell as the three of us go to Dad's car. Dad looks at me and says, "Sit in the back." Joe gives me the finger as he gets in the seat next to Dad. He's mad at me—Dad, I mean. He hates my hair. When Dad adjusts the rearview mirror, he looks at me and says, "Why did you have to cut it so short?"

"Because it's *my* hair," I say.

We drive down Main Street; Amanda is outside the shop giving directions to the guy who's setting up the new billboard. I roll down the window and yell, "Hey, Amanda." It takes her a second to recognize me and then waves back.

"Who's that?" Joe asks.

"It's the new Hortense."

"Oh, she's the one who did your hair?" Dad asks, as if offended.

"Yup, she's great. You would like her. She's really cool. She just moved here with her son. They're from Cincy. She's divorced."

Joe must be in a good mood because he pushes Dad with his elbow and says, "Hey, Dad, single girl in town. She is good-looking and seems about your age. Maybe you two . . ."

"Oh, yeah, Dad—I didn't think of that. Maybe I can introduce you . . ."

"Shut up, you two. It's your mom's birthday," Dad says dramatically, while still keeping an eye on Amanda.

Joe and I exchange looks and realize we took it a little too far. But then I push it even more. "Mom's dead, you know?" Joe shoots daggers at me with his eyes.

I expect the worst from Dad, but he simply nods and says, "To me, she's not dead."

I wanna say, "But she *is*," but I know better than

to open my mouth about Mom again, so I keep it to myself. Joe turns on the radio, but Dad turns it off in a second.

My mom's name was Alice. She met Dad when they were both in high school. They were just friends at first, but then they started dating when both of them were in community college, before Dad decided to join the Army. Their first year as a couple, Dad was stationed in Panama and Mom worked in Columbus at a day care. They would write to each other all the time. I have always wondered what happened to all those letters.

Dad became a disabled vet at a very young age. If you think about it, he retired when he was only twenty-something. Mom had had a couple of boyfriends, or so Elliot says, but Dad had only ever had one girlfriend and that was Mom.

"Dad proposed to Mom over the phone," Elliot told me once. Elliot says that Mom told Dad she wouldn't say anything until he was actually there to propose appropriately. At some point, Dad got leave from the Army and came home to ask Mom to marry him. He brought her a ring that he still keeps in his safe.

My parents got married in 1988. They didn't live together until Dad was stationed in Germany. He took my mom with him and they lived there for three years. There are lots of pictures of them in Europe. Life was great for them until Operation Desert Storm came along and Dad had to deploy. By then Mom was pregnant with Elliot so she came back to Ohio and lived with my grandparents.

"I was this close to being German," Elliot says all the time.

"But you ended up being a simple Londonian," Joe reminds him.

Less than two months after Dad's arrival in Saudi Arabia, he got shot in the leg and was sent back home. No more war for him. By then my grandfather was as sick and tired of the farm as Dad is now. That's how Dad ended up being in charge. Our family has lived here ever since.

Elliot says that Dad joined the Army to escape from the farm and make money, but while he was abroad it was the farm that he missed the most. Dad says that being injured was the worst and best thing that could have happened to him. It hurt a lot, but he got a pension and was still able to have a life, unlike some of his friends who were either so injured that they couldn't take care of themselves, or did not come back at all.

Dad's recovery was possible because of Mom. She would massage Dad's legs every night; she even learned how to do reflexology. She would also prepare salt baths every other day, and went to every single one of his appointments at the VA hospital. When Dad got depressed and decided to stay in bed, she was the one who forced him to get up and start physical therapy. I guess it was the teacher's spirit in her.

Mom worked in a preschool in downtown London. Half of the young adult population of London were once students of Mrs. Alice Jenkins.

Even today, when we're grocery shopping or selling at the farmers' market, we run into kids (well, they're not kids anymore), who introduce themselves as my mom's students. People say Mom was great with kids; she was the type of teacher everyone remembers. Dad says so, too. He's never gotten over her death. He may not talk about her all that much, but you know she's on his mind.

Actually, when I think about it, everything in our everyday life is a reminder of her. Our house is full of her photos. Alice Strawberries is more homage than product. Our walls, our decorations were Mom's work. Dad has never let us change a thing. Maybe we will live exactly the same way until someone else dies or someone else is born. It seems like deaths and births are the only factors of change in my family.

Births and deaths always come together for the Jenkins. See, a few months after my brother Elliot was born, our grandma died. A few weeks after Joe was born, my grandfather died. And well, our mom died right after I was born. It's some sort of curse; it's like tragedy follows our farm.

We spend the rest of the day *celebrating* Mom's birthday, which means paying respects at the cemetery, eating a steak at Mela's diner, and watching a game at home. Only Joe doesn't stay.

"I'm going out," he says.

"Where to?" Dad asks him.

"Nowhere. Just a short ride."

Joe goes for "short rides" a lot lately. His rides are anything but short. Sometimes we don't even hear him when he gets back.

"Don't come back too late, son."

"And if you do, don't make noise. You always wake us up," said Dad.

I grab an invisible knife and pass it along my neck from side to side behind Dad's back. Joe smiles and leaves.

Dad and I love watching football together. Or maybe it is just me who thinks this is our thing. As I said, Dad keeps everything to himself, except when it's about football. His emotions are all out when watching a game. Our team is the Bengals, obviously, but we both like the Ravens, too. There's something about younger teams that attracts us, I guess. We watch the whole game and during the break we eat pretzels and cheese for a snack. Dad drinks a beer and I drink a Dr. Pepper.

We don't talk all that much when we watch a game. Maybe only a few words like, "Did you see that?" and "No one can stop this guy, man!"

I enjoy it: it's really my favorite thing in life—after the farm, of course. Sometimes Jake comes and watches with us, but Dad thinks he talks way too much during the games. "He also makes way too much noise when he eats a pretzel," Dad says.

My old man acts like a seventy year old who gets annoyed at everything—light, darkness, sound, silence. It's hard to please him. There's no perfect moment with him: food is always missing spice; coffee is always missing sugar; soup is always missing water, oil, salt, who knows. I love him, though. He volunteers at the VA now and then, and he makes strawberry baskets for the shelter downtown. He has a good heart.

A commercial break comes on. Dad leans back in the sofa and looks at me—wait, no, he looks at my hair again. I see it coming, I see it coming . . .

"So, why did you cut your hair so short?"

"Because I like it, and because it's *my* . . . "

"It's *your* hair, I know."

"Say it already, say it. You hate it."

"It's not that, it's just . . . "

"What?"

"What if they start calling you *names* in school because of it?"

"Are you worried about Philip Carson calling me dyke again?"

"Well . . . "

"I punched him once, I can punch him again and again and again."

Dad is about to say something else, but the game is on again. The score is tied, sixteen to sixteen. I guess seeing the number makes my dad realize that my birthday is coming soon, because he says, "Hey, aren't you turning sixteen soon?"

"Yes, next weekend."

I will be sixteen. Sixteen is the number of years I have been without a mother. Sixteen is the number of years I have lived in London. Sixteen is the number of years I have lived in a body that I hate.

"What do you want?"

"I want the Bengals to win. That's what I want."

"No, I mean for your birthday. What do you want?"

If only I could say, "A hairy chest, a mustache, muscles, a dick." Instead I say, "I dunno. Money."

"How about clothes, how 'bout a dress?" he says.

I can't help it. I go, "What the fuck, Dad? When do I ever wear dresses?"

He gets mad and says that at sixteen, a girl should start dressing, behaving, and speaking like a lady.

I wanna punch Dad in the face, I swear. If Joe or Elliot were here they would say, "Come on, Dad.

Alex burps like a dude," and we would all laugh. But they're not here. They're never around when I need them the most.

I say, "Dad, I'm not a lady, I'm not Daddy's little girl. I'm a *kiddo*, understand? A *kiddo*."

"You're not a *kiddo*. You're my *daughter*, my *only* daughter."

"Why can't you just get it, Dad? I am who I am."

"You are who you are? And who *are* you, Alexandra?" he asks. I hate what he's doing. I hate it when he calls me Alexandra just to annoy me.

I say, "I am Alex and I am your fucking kid."

Dad ignores me, then says, "Go upstairs, you're interrupting me. Let me watch *my* game."

Now all of a sudden I'm interrupting him? He may as well say that I'm a girl, and girls don't understand football. Fuck that. I ignore him, and instead of doing what he tells me, I lean on the sofa and put my feet on the table. I say, "Come on, we're about to lose. You can't make me leave."

I can feel him staring at me and my hair for a

few seconds. Then he takes the remote, turns up the volume, and sits back.

When the game is over, we pick up everything from the table and walk to the kitchen. He pours himself some milk in a cup and asks me if I want some. I know I should drop the subject, but I go back to it.

"You've never cared about how I look. How come you care now?" I'm on fire now, "In fact, you were the one who started buying me boy's clothes, and now you wanna change?"

Dad looks at me. He sits down, takes a sip from his milk and says, "It's not that I want to change you. I'm just worried, Alex. I'm worried about you being bullied at school. I've read and heard about all these awful stories about kids that . . . "

"Let them try," I say. I hit my left palm with my right fist and make an angry face. Dad can't help it, he smiles.

"You are fucking crazy. *Crazy*," he says, then rubs his face with his hands and yawns. "I'm tired. I'm off to bed. Let's hope your brother doesn't make a lot of noise when he comes in late."

"Where do you think he goes, Dad?"

"Who knows? Your brother is a mystery, even more than you are. Turn off the lights, will you?" he asks. Before leaving the kitchen, Dad kisses me on the forehead. He doesn't say, *I love you.*

"Night, Dad."

I clean up the kitchen a little bit, open the fridge, and get ham and cheese to make a sandwich. I decide to eat it in the living room and watch TV just for a little while. A few minutes later, I hear Joe coming in. He slams the door. "Shh, Dad's sleeping." He ignores me. He throws his keys and his jacket on the sofa.

"Hey, you okay?" I ask him.

"Don't ask."

"What is it?" Today I don't even get, "Mind your own business, Alex."

He goes to the kitchen, opens a beer, takes a long sip, and then goes upstairs. I wonder what is going on with him.

* * *

I wake the next morning. It's Monday, but there is no school today. Teacher conferences or something. I wake up early and work with Dad outside until we both feel hungry.

Dad and I start making sandwiches together. Dad calls Joe and asks him to help out. But Joe ignores him. Dad calls Joe three, four, five times. Finally Joe comes in. He's mad.

"What is it, Joe?" Dad asks.

"Nothing."

"He's been like that since last night," me and my big mouth say.

"Shut up. Nobody asked you, you idiot."

"Joseph!"

Sparks start flying. Joe and Dad start arguing. I

take my sandwich to my room and leave them to solving their shit.

The yelling goes on and on, so I finish eating, wash up, put on my clothes, and go out.

I take my bike and ride. For a second I stop outside Jake's. I kinda feel like going in and puking all these emotions on his bed, but Jake is probably hanging out with his family so I decide not to interrupt.

Sometimes I wonder what it would be like, you know, to have a perfect family. One thing leads to another and all the many memories of us as the most imperfect family in town show up. I start feeling mad, thinking about the family I don't have, the person I'm not. I start pedaling faster and faster. My legs are trying to help me let go of all this frustration.

I don't even realize I am heading downtown until I get there.

"Hey stranger!" Amanda yells at me. I stop my bike and ride slowly to her.

"Hey," I reply.

"You're riding your ass off. Are you okay?" she asks as she touches me by the shoulder.

"I'm fine. It's just my family is having this big fight at home. They drive me crazy."

"Well, that's exactly what families do—drive everyone crazy. What fun would life be if we didn't have that?" Amanda laughs. "What are you up to?"

I shrug and point at the Baskin Robbins sign.

Amanda smiles and says, "Oh, yes, what's the point of being mad if you can't have ice cream, right? Can I join you?"

As Amanda and I walk into the store, I see a kid with pink hair. I'm starting to realize he's George, Amanda's son, when he goes, "Jesus, Amanda, can't I have a moment alone?"

Amanda sticks out her tongue and walks over to George. She takes the spoon out of his hand and says, "Mmm, Banana Split?" She tries each of the three flavors, then looks at me. "This is Alex. She goes to your school."

George looks me up and down. He studies me for a long time and finally says, "Hey."

I order my ice cream. Amanda orders a milkshake.

George jokes with Amanda and tells her to at least sit at a different table, but she refuses. "I'm sitting with my loving son," she says and she sits next to him. They argue for a bit, and then they make peace.

Amanda asks me to sit down with them. Both start asking me questions. They wanna know all about London and its people. I tell them about our mayor and how she used to sell cookies and cupcakes at Christmas long before she turned to politics. I tell them all the weird, funny, and creepy stories I know about my town. We have a good time.

At some point Amanda leaves and George and I start talking about school and shit. He wants to know everything about our teachers and our classmates. It's late when we say goodbye. I ride back home feeling totally refreshed. I liked hanging out with them, but especially, I liked talking to George.

At home, things look better than before. Joe and Dad are watching a Chuck Norris movie.

"Where were you?" Dad asks me.

I see him and I realize what I want for my birthday. I want Amanda to meet my dad and for them to fall in love. Amanda would become my stepmother and life would be so much easier.

I'm not stupid. I know that's not gonna happen. One, because Dad's a brick with no emotions. Two, because life isn't like in the movies. Three, because birthday wishes never come true. And four, because according to George, his mom would never get married again after what happened with George's dad.

Although he didn't tell me the whole story, what I understood is that his dad was violent, one of those alcoholics who are super nice during the day and beasts at night. Plus, he was ashamed of George being gay. In George's words, "My old man tried to punch the gayness out of me and Mom stopped him."

*   *   *

When the Chuck Norris movie is over, I say, "Good Night," to Dad and Joe and I go to my room. I text Jake and tell him I met a kid who should become our friend. No reply. I put on my PJs and jump in bed. It's still early but I'm tired. I close my eyes and fall asleep right away.

I dream that Amanda washes my hair. It feels wonderful. I don't know what she does, but my head didn't feel this way with Hortense. I'm at peace. It's like as she cleans my hair, she clears my mind. All my fears rinse away. We don't talk. She's just there, washing my hair and my thoughts.

When Amanda finishes, she points me to the chair. I sit down and when I see myself in the mirror I am older. I am like twenty-something and I have a big mustache. She asks, "So, Alex, how's family? How's the wife?"

* * *

We are celebrating my birthday one day early because Dad's going to a fair in Illinois. I suggested we go to Mela's diner, but he went fancy. We're at the The Grill Steak House. I love this place, and Dad knows it.

"It's your sweet sixteen after all," he says.

"More like a charcoal sixteen," I say, and we all laugh.

I have invited Jake. We eat and talk and eat and talk. When we are waiting for dessert, Dad says, "It's time for presents."

Joe gives me a sports watch and Jake gives me a Gillian Flynn novel. He knows how much I love suspense. Dad's gift ends the happiness of the moment. He gives me a dress. Yes, a dress. Just as he said he would.

I look at it, I look at him and I have no clue what to say. Joe reads my mind and says, "Really, Dad? A dress?"

Jake tries to make the moment less awkward and says, "Wow, perfect for the October Ball."

Dad says nothing at first. Then he hands me the receipt and says, "If it doesn't fit you, or if you don't like it, just exchange it." He stands up and goes to ask for the check. Joe and Jake look at me. They are waiting for me to say something. But I say nothing; I put the dress on the side and take Jake's gift. I read the first line:

I have a meanness inside me, real as an organ.

I don't think I have a meanness inside me, I just think I have a boy inside me, real and with organs. And this boy, my boy inside me would never wear a dress.

CHAPTER FIVE
a Different Kind of girl

MY ACTUAL BIRTHDAY IS A BIT . . . WHATEVER. JAKE and I watched a movie at his place and that was it. The plan is to spend the rest of the weekend studying because midterms are here. We're frying our brains with problems and lines and numbers, and while we're at it, we try to overdose on junk food.

"I should have invited George to study with us. Is it too late to call him?" I ask with my mouth full of Raisinets.

"George talks too much. Besides, he's too *flamboyant*," Jake snarls, then he takes a sip of his Mountain Dew.

"Do you even know what that word means?" I ask.

"Of course I do. It's a euphemism that I used instead of saying that George is *too gay*, which I can't say. If I did, you would say I'm homophobic and I'm not."

"So you mind that George's *too gay*, but you're not homophobic? How's that work?"

Jake's been a little weird since I started hanging out with George. It's like he's jealous. That's so stupid. George is cool, yes, and I really dig him, but Jake, well, Jake's always been and will always be in my life.

They're so different. George gets me in ways Jake can't, sometimes even more than Jake.

"I don't mind that he's gay. Hell, he can even prefer cows over women and men for all I care. It's just that he's out of the closet way too much and becomes a target for everyone at school," Jake replies as if what he's saying makes sense.

"Well, he doesn't seem to mind. Didn't you hear

what he told Philip Carson after he made fun of George's new hair-do?"

"Didn't *you* see how that asshole punched him after that?" Jake replies.

"Well, I like George and I think he's brave and authentic. He's honest. I like that he doesn't try to hide who he is."

"Unlike you, you mean?"

I don't know how to react or what to say. I stand up, my hands shaking until my mind catches up to his words. I push his books away and tell him to fuck off.

"Hey, I'm working. What's wrong with you?" he says as he picks up his notebook and pen from the floor.

"What's wrong with me? You *are* what's wrong with me."

"Alex, come on. It was a joke."

"You're a fucking asshole, you know that?"

"Jesus, now I can't even joke? What's gotten into you? You're in a bad mood all the fucking time."

I start getting my shit together, so willing to leave, but he won't let me.

"Come on, Alex, don't get mad. Stay, we have so much to do."

I look at him. I wanna go, but at the same time, I really do need his help studying. I sit back on the chair and mumble, "Fine."

We work for a while and then Jake says, "The thing is, Alex. You don't have to hide who you are. You are just a *different kind of girl*, period."

"Oh, my God, cut it out, will you?"

I go back to my notes and take the remote out of his hands so I can turn up the volume of the music. We're listening to Lorde's "Pure Heroine." This is exactly what Dad does when he doesn't wanna talk. Music, TV, anything but a normal conversation.

Jake and I continue working, and then he starts in again, "Do you like someone at school?"

I reply, "*Different kind of girl* does not like anyone at school, thank you very much."

Jake takes it and turns down the volume. He goes, "No, I mean, do you like-like someone?"

"No. No one. You?" I ask as I grab the remote again. He seems disappointed. It isn't the first time he has asked me this. He's been beating around the bush for a while now. He stands up, takes the remote, and turns the music player off. He sits right in front of me on the dining room table and asks, "Alex, do you like boys?"

"Whaddya mean?"

"Or do you like girls?" He's looking at me, waiting for an answer.

"Boys, of course," I lie.

Well, no. I don't lie. I just don't know what to say. I mean, I do like boys. I like every one of the guys on our football team. I like their bodies; I like looking at them when they play football shirtless near my farm in summer. Only I don't like them like that. I just like to look at them.

"Are you sure?" Jake insists. Why is he asking me this? Why are we even talking about it?

"Yes. Now can you turn on the music, please? That's my favorite song and you know it."

Jake turns it on and sits next to me. After a while he goes, "Alex, you know . . . you know you can tell me anything, right?"

I look up. "What the fuck has gotten into you? Ever since you and Maggie broke up you've been acting weird. Look, if you don't wanna work and help me with this, that's fine. But I have to study, so I am gonna go." I grab my backpack and this time I'm serious—I'm walking to the door.

"Alex, wait. It's okay if you're a *different kind of girl.*"

"Stop with that *different kind of girl* shit. Lesbian. Lesbian is what you wanna say, right?"

"I guess," he looks at me, and then adds, "So are you? Are you a lesbian, Alex?"

"Fuck off."

I slam the door and leave.

I end up studying on my own the rest of the

weekend. Happy Birthday to me. Fucking midterms. Fucking Jake.

* * *

If trying not to fail isn't hard enough, I'm once again being sent to the school's counselor because of my attitude problems.

"I don't have any attitude problem," I tell Mrs. Smith. "If anything, the one who has an attitude problem is Philip Carson. Me? I just don't like people."

She asks me if that includes Jake. I explain that Jake is different. He's actually my friend. "He likes me the way I am," I tell her. But, actually, I'm not sure if that is even true anymore, considering our fight.

"Alex? What do you mean by *the way you are*? What is that?"

I try to explain myself but she just doesn't get it. She says something about being okay if I feel I am a *different* kind of girl. Translation: It is okay if you are a lesbian—that's what she is trying to say. So now I am just here, listening to her blabbing about diversity and shit.

When the bell rings, she says, "Remember Alex, it's okay to be different. You're just a *different kind of girl.*"

Same thing Jake said. The reason we fought.

"You know it's okay if you like girls, right?" George says. We're walking to his place after school. I'm telling him all about Jake and my conversation with Mrs. Smith. George mentions Tina and Rose, the "lesbian lovebirds" as everyone calls them, a senior couple from our school. I tell him that I see regular girls in them.

"Regular girls don't make out with each other," says George.

"Well, but they look like regular girls who don't

wanna ruin their nails." We laugh. I tell him that I tried hanging out with Tina, Rose and some of their friends last semester, since we all were on the track team.

"And? What happened? You're not friends anymore?"

"No, not really. Maggie didn't like them all that much."

"Maggie?"

"Yeah."

George stops for a second. He looks at me and asks, "Who the fuck is Maggie and what the fuck does Maggie have to do with all this?"

"Jake's girlfriend, I mean ex-girlfriend. You've seen her around, I'm sure. She was my friend then too and, well, she didn't like Tina and Rose. She didn't want me hanging out with them," I say.

"*What?* You stopped being friends with them because Maggie asked you to? Are you serious? Who's she to tell you what to do?" I hear what

George is saying and as I review his words, I realize that, indeed, it all sounds wrong.

"I know it sounds weird, but Maggie, Jake and I, well, we were all friends and . . . "

"Oh my God, Alex . . . This sounds like a love triangle. I think this Maggie person likes *you*. Sounds to me like she was just as jealous as Jake is right now."

"You don't know what you're talking about, George, it's not like that . . . I mean, you don't even know her."

"Well, now I want to. Alex, believe me. I'm always right. I think Maggie . . . wait, why did she and Jake break up?"

I shrug.

"Anyway, it's not like I wanted to be friends with Tina and Rose. I actually felt out of touch around them. It's like they're lesbians just to show off, just to get everyone's attention." I fold up the sleeves of my t-shirt, place my hands on my pocket and say,

"Hey, look at me, I'm a lesbian and I'm not afraid of you sissies."

George laughs and says, "You are such a dick."

I tell him, "As I always say, better a dick than a dyke."

"I hate that word. I hate it. I hate fag, too. The only person allowed to call me a fag is me." George opens up. "I've been hearing it since I was a kid. How is it that before kids can spell, they know words like fag and dyke and . . . "

"Were you always . . . did you always know that you . . . ?" The moment I start the question I realize I don't even know how to ask what I wanna ask.

"That I am a fag?" George's voice is louder. The subject makes him angry.

"No, no, that's not what I was going to say. Fuck, George, I'm sorry. I have no right to . . . " George laughs, grabs me by my shoulders and shakes me.

"Relax, Alex, *relax*." His hands come down my arms and find my hands. He holds them tight. "Yes, I have always been a fag, only I didn't know exactly what that meant. My dad used to say that it was all my mom's fault, for raising me at the beauty parlor, but he was wrong. I am what I am just . . . just because."

"Just because?" I ask. I'm intrigued.

"What do you want me to explain that you don't already know? I mean, you've probably gone through the same shit. Everyone making fun of you because you're not like the other girls, because you wanna be a farmer. That happens to me. I'm not *one of the boys*. Everyone laughed at me because I preferred Dora the Explorer to Max Steel. Although, between you and me, I wanked many times with handsome Max Steel on my mind."

"TMI, George—I don't need to know that!"

We've arrived at George's place. He takes me to his bedroom. It's only my second time here. It takes time to adjust to the place. There are too many things to look at. He's got posters of fashion models all over his walls. He has a lot of books, most of them about design, fashion, and photography. He says he wants to work in the fashion industry. I can picture him as a host of Fashion Emergency. It sort of reminds me of my brother, Elliot. Both are the achiever kind.

"It's okay to talk about it Alex. I think you need to talk about it. I see you struggling."

"Struggling?"

"Struggling to be yourself. Man, you are always in such a bad mood."

"Argh, Jake says the same thing. I don't know . . . "

"That's exactly the problem. You don't know, but it's okay, you can know now."

"Know what?" I ask him.

"Know that you are gay, know that you are *different* . . . "

"What is it with you and your mom? Both of you are, you guys are . . . " I don't even know what to say.

"We care about you. We both do. I mean, my mom cares about everybody because she is a hairdresser-slash-therapist, but me, I believe I came to this fucking town to meet you and help you . . . "

"What, am I like your mission in life or some bullshit like that?"

"Ha ha, you can be funny when you're mad."

"I have to go." I stand up and try to leave.

"Wait, don't. Don't go, Alex—not like that. Look, maybe we're wrong, maybe you're just a girl who likes guy's stuff and shit, and that is okay too, but I have gaydar, you know? And I think you are gay and you know it, but you don't want to admit it to yourself."

"Shut up! Shut up!" I yell at George as I begin to cry. What is it with them? George and Amanda move me in so many ways. I never cry. I never ever cry but with them I feel so vulnerable.

"Alex, there's nothing worse than lying to yourself and, forgive me if I'm wrong, but I think that is exactly what you're doing. If you are a lesbian, it's okay. I think that's what Jake was trying to tell you."

"You don't know what you talking about!" George tries to hug me but I push him away and say, "I'm not a lesbian, I'm not. I . . . I . . . I'm a boy. I wanna be a boy," I finally say.

George stares at me. "What are you saying, Alex?" He walks back to his bed and sits down. He stays quiet for a bit while he looks at me, trying to figure me out. I have felt that look before. I remember all the other times when people realize I'm not a boy: the spell breaks and I turn into a frog. Only now, now I'm really a frog, an ugly frog who was born a girl but is actually a boy.

George finally says, "Well, it's even worse than I imagined."

"Worse? You think?!" I ask as I dry my eyes with a corner of my shirt.

"Or better, who knows? Come, sit with me."

I start telling George that when I was in elementary school, Jake and I were running around during recess, playing gladiators, when this kid from fifth grade came and made fun of us. He called me a dyke. That was a new word for me. I had been called a tomboy so many times, that it didn't bother me anymore. But dyke was new. "It's not what it means so much as the fact that people use it as an insult."

He agrees with me.

"If I had a quarter for every time someone called me dyke, I would be rich by now. Okay, maybe I'm exaggerating. It's just I *hate* that word. Plus, I am not a dyke. Believe me I would have no trouble admitting it if I was a lesbian . . . I would even say, 'Hi, my name is Alex. I am a lesbian and wannabe farmer.'"

"Dude, come on, I'm sure you wouldn't say that," George laughs.

"What do you think you know?"

"Oh, I know. I've seen you. You walk around so proud and tough in school, but at the same time you are ashamed. You wanna be invisible."

George's right. I wanna be invisible. I wanna disappear. I wanna go away. I wanna go away and then come back the way I was supposed to be. I wanna come back as a boy.

"Dad wanted me to be a girl. Without noticing, he ended up raising me to be a farmer, and I have always worked my ass off as much as my brothers to keep things running around the farm. I even find time to help Jake with his chores at his parents' farm. I don't see why everyone has a problem with me being the way I am." I am lying on my back on George's bed.

He is by my side. He doesn't say anything for a moment, then tells me something I had never thought of before, "Well, it's not that everyone has a problem with you being the way you are. *You* have a problem being the way you are."

"But, what am I, George, what am I? I was born a girl, I know. But I don't like it. No one accepts me as a girl. I wish I was born a boy."

"What would you do if you could make your wish come true?" George asks.

"That's stupid, I can't be a boy!" I yell and push him off the bed.

"Just think about it. Use your imagination. No one can blame you for fantasizing. What would you do if you were a boy?"

A thousand ideas fly through my mind. I have so many things to say that I don't even know where to start.

"I . . . I . . . I would have a farm. I would have horses and chickens and would grow more than strawberries. I would have a huge jeep and would ride everywhere in it. I . . .I would have a girlfriend, a girlfriend who would love the inside boy I think I am."

Everything disappears for a second and I'm not in George's bedroom anymore. I see myself lying down next to the lake. It's only me and my jeep and my girlfriend. I have a hairy face and I walk out of my barn with no shirt because it is too hot.

I start crying again. George sits up on the bed and pulls me to his lap. He caresses my hair like Amanda did in my dream.

"What am I going to do, George?" I ask.

"I don't know, Alex, but we'll figure it out. I promise."

I close my eyes and let myself be soothed by George, when suddenly he shakes my shoulders and yells, "Oh, I know what I'm gonna give you as a birthday present."

"My birthday was last week."

"I know, but a present is a present, and you'll love mine. You'll see."

* * *

Everyone in school is at the gym for an assembly. I'm sitting alone and looking for Jake, who didn't knock on my door this morning so we could ride together. I see him walking through the door and I wave to him to come and sit with me. He hesitates. It takes him a few seconds to decide if he should come or not. He finally does, but before he sits down, he says, "Are you going to be an asshole again?"

"Shut up and sit down. I'm always gonna be an asshole."

Jake laughs and joins me on the bleachers.

"So, any fight worth talking about, my dear troublemaker?" he asks.

"No. But it's still early. Ask me again at lunch." Jake laughs. I look at him and I see the little boy he used to be, the boy I've grown up with.

"I'm really sorry about the other day."

He frowns at me.

"I know you were just trying to talk and shit . . . I was thinking, how about riding to the lake after school? I really need to talk to you."

"What about?" Jake replies as he takes a Snickers out of his backpack.

"Man, how can you eat that at eight in the morning?"

"Breakfast of champions." He swallows a huge part of his Snickers and asks, "So, what'd you wanna talk about. You okay?"

"Kinda. There's something I wanna talk to you about."

The principal takes the microphone and starts telling us about the events our school has planned for October. He introduces the students who will be planning the Halloween dance at the end of the month. George is president of the party committee. After the principal introduces him, George waves to everyone like a queen to her subjects.

"You should ask your friend to get us free tickets for the dance," Jake says.

"Do you wanna go?"

"Sure, why not?" Jake says as he pulls out two lollipops from his pack and hands me one. "We should go together."

"You're nuts. There's no way I would go to that."

"Come on, Alex. It could be fun. Whaddya say?"

Jake places his hand on my hand and smiles. I don't know what to think of this. This is not the way we usually are with each other. I move my hand away and say, "We'll see."

The principal dismisses us to our second period classes. Jake and I stand up and as we walk out of the gym a voice yells, "Look, it's Alexander Jenkins and his girlfriend Jake-leen." It's stupid Philip Carson.

"Ignore him. Let's just go to class," Jake says.

Philip continues, "Looks like girlfriend doesn't want Mr. Alex to get in trouble . . . "

"Fuck off, Philip," I say and keep walking with Jake by my side. All of a sudden Jake and I get pulled away from the crowd and surrounded by Philip and his friends.

"My parents took away my phone. You know why? Because of what happened the other day. Mrs. Smith called. Told them I was harassing a girl in school."

"Poor you," I say. "I wonder why you don't have a girlfriend?"

"Shut the fuck up."

"Let her go, Carson," Jake intervenes.

"Mind your own business," snaps Philip pushing Jake to the floor.

"Leave Jake out of this!" I yell before hitting him right in his face.

Philip touches his mouth. He's bleeding. He looks at Jake, still on the floor, and says, "Man, you chose a good boyfriend. Looks like *he* fights for you."

"What's going on there?" one of the teachers yell. Philip takes off. Jake stands up and also hurries away.

"Jake, wait up."

"Damn it, Alex. You made me look like a pussy."

"Are you serious? Look, if I hadn't hit him . . . "

"You don't think I can take care of myself? Just let me go. I'll be late for class."

As Jake walks away, I yell, "Are we still on for the lake?"

"Whatever."

I lose him in the crowd of students. I feel alone in the huge open space of the gymnasium.

"Alex, you okay?"

It's Maggie. I turn around and see her standing there.

"Yeah, it's just Jake. We're fighting all the time lately."

"I'm sorry. I guess it's my fault."

"Your fault? Why, because you guys broke up?"

Maggie shrugs.

"Nah, it's not because of that. Jake is just . . . he's just weird, I guess. We all are."

"I know," Maggie says, and then she waves goodbye.

CHAPTER SIX
coming out

I WAIT FOR JAKE OUTSIDE SCHOOL. I STAND RIGHT next to his bike. The second I see him, I ask, "So, the lake?"

"If you want," he replies indifferently. He takes the lock off his bike.

"We haven't been in a while. Come on, we can't be like this anymore—we've been like dogs and cats lately. We need a lake moment."

Jake smiles and says, "I take it you're the dog, right?"

"Yeah, and I'll bite you if you don't come along."

"Fine," he answers.

Jake and I started going to the lake on our own

when we were seven years old. It was hard to convince our parents that it was safe, that nothing was going to happen to us, that we would not do anything too crazy. Truth is, I have no idea why they allowed us to go, because by then, we had already gotten into so much trouble together.

Back then we just took off our shirts and jumped in the lake wearing nothing but our shorts. The first time I did it, Jake said, "Don't you have a swimsuit?" I looked at him in his blue speedo. "Why do I need a swimsuit?" It seemed that my answer was good enough for him because he didn't say anything else. Plus, our bodies looked the same—why did I have to cover it up?

Nevertheless, Debbie, Jake's mom, disagreed. One day she came to the lake to check on us. I was about to dive off the pier when she asked me the same question: did I have a swimsuit?

"But I don't need one," I told her.

"Well, you do, sweetie. Girls and boys have different bodies and . . . "

With my hands on my waist, I said, "Jake and I have the same bodies." Jake stood up and showed his chest off above the water.

Debbie looked at us, smiled, and covered me with a towel. "Well, Alexandra, now they look the same but they are not the same and as you both grow up . . . "

I interrupted her and said, "I know, I know, I will have boobs. But I don't want them . . . " I took the towel off and ran back to the water; Jake did the same. What could Debbie do?

* * *

We ride to the lake without saying a word. I know he's still upset because of what happened earlier with Philip, so I give him time to cool off. As we pass our houses we run into Debbie on the street.

"What are you up to?" she asks while getting into her car.

"Going to the lake," I say. "Just for a bit."

"With this weather? You guys are crazy." She is right. It's chilly out here. "I'm going to the store. Alex, you eating with us tonight?" Debbie asks.

"No, Alex is having dinner with her family, Mom," Jake replies.

"Wow, now *you* answer for me? What if the highlight of my day is having dinner with you guys?" I scoff.

"Well, since *you* fight for me, I thought answering for you would be no big deal," Jake replies. It's clear as day that he's still pissed.

"Fight?" Debbie asks, looking at us.

"Nothing. Never mind, Mom," Jake tells her.

"Go on to the lake already and don't come back late," Debbie says before waving goodbye.

Debbie has always tried to be close to me, to be a role model. She hasn't done so well, though. She was never able to convince me to be more feminine, not to mention to wear dresses or skirts. I think by now she has lost all hope.

A few days after our conversation at the lake,

she bought me a red swimsuit and some matching sandals. "But, but . . . " I liked the bright red of the fabric but my cutoffs were working just fine. What was the big deal?

"No buts. You're a girl and need to wear a swimsuit if you guys are planning to spend all summer at the lake." I nodded but felt unconvinced. "I also talked to your dad and I will be taking you shopping before school starts. We need to get you out of your brothers' clothes."

Elliot says that when I was little, Dad didn't know exactly what to buy me from the girls department, and since in London we pretty much have only two seasons: summer and winter, he always bought a bunch of shorts and t-shirts for the summer and a bunch of pants and hoodies for the winter. And, of course, when my brothers outgrew their clothes, these were passed on to me.

Shopping with Debbie wasn't fun. I would show her something I liked and she would say no. She would show me something she found and I would say no. Her intentions were good. She was just worried I would not develop a feminine vibe as I got older.

Debbie has always told me I can confide in her and talk to her about anything I want: "You know, boys, clothes, cramps." Yeah, because that's *exactly* what I wanna talk about.

I shouldn't be so harsh. Debbie has really tried to be, if not a mother figure, at least an aunt for me. When I got my first period, guess whom I ran to? Debbie, of course.

Finally, we arrive at the lake. We consider the lake *ours*. It's not London's lake. It is Alex and Jake's. We hadn't been here since the summer, when we were hanging out here with Maggie. Jake's been moody lately. It seems that every time we're having a good time, we find a way to fuck it up by arguing. Also, since I met George I've been hanging out with him more than I have with Jake. I wonder if he feels left out.

We both climb off our bikes and walk out on

the pier. As we sit down, Jake takes out a bag of M&Ms, the peanut kind.

"God, Jake, did you go trick or treating early this year or what? You've been eating a lot of candy lately."

"Daphne's been going to so many birthday parties and it seems like the trend with her classmates is to have *piñatas*. Since Mom doesn't let her eat candy . . . "

"I see."

"Want some?"

"No, thanks. I'm watching my diet," I scoff.

"Whatever," he says. I watch him finish the M&Ms in less than a minute. I take a sip from my water bottle and think about how to start this conversation.

"So . . . "

"So?" Jake says as he looks for something in his backpack.

"First, let's talk about today."

"About the fact that you made me look like a pussy who can't fight on his own?"

"Come on, Jake. It was not like that and you know it."

"Well, that's how it felt, Alex."

"I'm sorry, then. I'll let Philip Carson kick your ass next time."

"You're such an idiot. See what you are saying?"

"What?!"

"You don't think I am capable of kicking Carson's ass. You automatically assume he's going to win."

"That's not what I said, you didn't even let me finish my sentence. What I was trying to say is . . . "

"Forget it, Alex. I know I can't kick ass like you do."

"Okay, for the record, you said that, not me."

"Whatever. Anyway, I am glad you wanted to come here to talk. I also have something to tell you."

Jake turns and crosses his legs to sit in front of me.

"Wait, Jake. I haven't even finished my part."

"It's okay, you can tell me after. This can't wait."

"But . . . "

He glares at me. "You owe me that much."

"Fine. Go."

Jake fixes his eyes on me and then closes them for a second. He looks at the lake and takes a deep breath. He looks nervous. I don't understand what is going on. Jake is weirder than usual.

"Remember when I told you back in the summer that Maggie and I had broken up?"

"Yup. I also remember that when I asked you what had happened you told me to fuck off."

"Did I?"

"Yup. But we can talk about it now . . . if you want."

"You don't mind?"

"Why would I?"

"I dunno, maybe it's weird for you hearing me talk about this other girl who was in my life and . . . "

"Gee, Jake, you sound like your mother."

"My mother?"

"Yes, Debbie asked me more than once if I was okay about you two guys being together. I kept telling her it was all cool, but she wasn't convinced. Maybe she thought I would get jealous. Can you believe it?"

"So . . . you weren't ever jealous?"

"Of you dating Maggie? Of course not, silly. You and I will always be friends. No matter what. No matter how many women come into your life. We are best friends—BFFs."

"So much for a BFF."

"What you mean?"

"First you didn't really care about me and Maggie breaking up, then . . . "

"I did, too! I totally cared. Maybe I just didn't show it."

"You didn't."

I take a big breath and then say, "Well, to be honest, I was kinda happy you guys broke up, but I wasn't going to say that, of course."

Jake looks at me puzzled and right away asks, "Happy? Why were you happy?"

"God, that probably made me sound like a douche. I don't mean happy-happy. I mean . . . well, you know."

"No, I don't. Explain." Jake is all serious. I don't think I have seen him like this.

"Well . . . " I start.

"Just spit it out, Alex."

"Oh my God. Are you on your period or what?" I say. Big mistake.

"Because I am a pussy, right?"

"No, man. That's not . . . I didn't . . . " It seems like whatever I say will sink me deeper into my own shit. As I try to come up with the right words, Jake takes the initiative and says, "Alex, I love you."

I don't even think about it and answer back, "Jake, I love you, too. You know that."

"No, Alex. You don't understand. I love you-love you, like *I am in love with you.*"

What the fuck? This isn't happening. Please, this isn't happening.

The lake is empty, there's no one around. That's why this had always been the perfect place for us since we were kids. We would swim, fish, dive, run, jump. It was the perfect place to play war.

Jake had a big collection of plastic soldiers. So he would pack his soldiers, and I would pack my cars and tanks and off we would go to create battles right next to the water, which in our eyes became a huge ocean. Forget the Normandy Invasion, we masterminded the London Invasion. My troops against his: to defend London's inhabitants from an evil enemy.

We even started wearing pieces of Dad's old uniform. I would wear his cap, and Jake would wear the jacket, or vice versa. It really didn't matter. Sometimes I was the enemy that traveled by sea to make slaves out of the people of London.

I don't know when exactly we exchanged the soldiers for superhero comics or when going to the lake became just lying on the deck and watching the sky. As we grew up, the lake became more of a sanctuary than a playground. It became the place we chose to be when things in our homes were not so pleasant. But now, now the lake was anything but a comfort zone.

"Hello! Alex? Did you hear me?" Jake waves at me, trying to snap me out of my thoughts.

"I did, Jake, but . . . "

"But?"

"Huh? Come on, Jake, we're friends. We have always been friends."

"And? That's exactly the best part of it. We know everything about each other. Everyone has always thought we would end up together."

"If by everyone you mean the people from school . . . " I stand up. "Listen, I should go. I need—*we* need some time to think."

"Alex, you can't go. Come on! Do you have any idea how hard it was for me to tell you this?"

"Jake, please, stop."

"You love me too. I know it." Jake has always been a little dramatic. I blame it on the drama club and the TV shows that he watches. It's like there's a script in his mind that influences him.

"No, Jake. I don't love you. Not like that. You are my dearest friend. We grew up like brother and sister. Actually. . . " I know I have to tell him. I have to tell him now. Just say it. "Not like brother and sister. More like brother and brother. I want you to see me as your brother." There, I said it; I fucking finally said it.

"What the hell are you talking about, Alex?"

"I, I don't like men . . . "

"What? Goddamnit, Alex—did you lie to me then? I asked you—I asked you just the other day if you liked boys or girls. I told you it was okay if you liked girls, but you said, you specifically said you liked boys. Don't you remember?"

"I do. I mean, I do remember. I know I said that, but it was only because . . . "

"Because what? You changed your mind?" Jake's face is changing from red to purple.

"Because I didn't know! I really didn't! I just know that I have always felt different and . . . See, I talked to George the other day and . . . "

"George? You talked about this with him first? How can you even trust that fag?"

"Don't you dare call him that."

"It's the truth. He's a fag and you . . . You are a dyke."

He's gone too far. I push Jake away. I push him as hard as I can.

He falls on the deck.

"I am not a dyke. Don't you ever call me that! Don't you ever tell me that you are in love with me. You don't know what you're talking about. You're just confused."

Jake stands up and says, "I don't know what *I'm* talking about? You serious? The only one who has always been confused is you, Alexandra."

It's the very first time since we met that Jake has

called me Alexandra in a serious conversation. The only other times he used my whole name was when we were goofing around in the woods.

"JAKE SHERIDAN, YOU HOOOOME??"

"YES, ALEXANDRA JENKINS, I AM HOME!!!"

But today, today Jake is calling me Alexandra just to make me mad, like he's trying to prove a point.

"Fuck you, Jake. Fuck you." I move and try to hit him again but he covers his face, which gives me a chance to say, "You see, if I am a dyke, then you are a pussy. A pussy who's afraid of being hit in the face." I race from the pier and jump on my bike.

I wish I could fucking cry, but I can't. I'm too angry for that. As I ride back home I think of everything that's happened today. I think back on everything that has been said between us in the last couple of months. How could I not see it? What I had planned to be my coming out to my best friend turned into something else.

When I get home, my plan is to go directly to

the kitchen and eat whatever is there, but when I arrive I see my dad talking on the phone, all serious. Joe is right next to him. Something is going on. Joe notices my clueless face and he whispers, "It's Elliot, he had an accident."

CHAPTER SEVEN
man out

I FEEL TRAPPED AT HOME. I WALK AROUND MY ROOM, trying to organize it just as a distraction. I look at myself in the mirror, my hair is a bit of a mess. Or maybe it's just that I want an excuse to go visit Amanda. I text her, she replies right away and says she can do my hair in half an hour. I get dressed. I grab some money, put on my sneakers, and get ready to go.

As I close the front door, I see Jake working on his bike. He doesn't even look at me. I climb on my bike and ride downtown.

As I get on Main I run into Maggie. She's talking with a bunch of people, fucking Philip Carson included. I thought she didn't like him. She smiles and waves at me. Carson says some stupid shit and Maggie pushes him.

I ride all the way to Amanda's, just a couple of blocks from Maggie and her friends. I park my bike and she is already there, greeting me at the door. "My favorite client!" she says. She immediately notices something is wrong with me, and says, "You come for a haircut or to have some Amanda time?"

I smile and say, "I came for both."

She takes me by the hand and sits me down to wash my hair. She says nothing for a while. She softly massages my hair and my scalp. The feeling of the warm water and the tenderness of her hands make me wanna cry. I feel like shit. It's like everything around me is changing.

When she's done washing my hair she takes me to the mirror. I sit down and she starts combing my hair, but stops suddenly. She looks at me in the mirror, then turns my chair to her and sits next to me. She stares at me.

"What? Why are you looking at me like that?"

Amanda breathes in deep and exhales slowly. She leans over and rests her hands on my knees.

"What's going on, Alex?"

"Nothing," I lie.

But Amanda looks at me as if saying, *Do you think you can fool me?*

I take a big breath and say, "It's just, everything is going to hell. My older brother is in the hospital, my best friend went fucking nuts, I'm confused, and I'm a mess. My life is a mess." I decide to add something funny, "A mess, just like my hair."

Amanda looks at me and says, "I'm sorry about your brother. He's the one in the army, right?"

"Yeah, Elliot. He's in intensive care. My dad is with him now."

"I'm sorry to hear that. What happened?"

"We don't know exactly. It was an accident during training, and now he's got burns all over."

"Jesus." Amanda rubs my thigh. It's like she's

saying, *It will be all right.* She smiles and says, "What else is going on with you, Alex?"

I shrug and say, "Dunno, I'm a mess."

Amanda looks at me in the mirror. "I'm going to ask you something very personal." Amanda's eyes watch me. "You don't have to answer if you don't want to."

"Okay . . . ," I say making a face like I really have no idea what she's going to ask. But I know, oh, I know, what she's going to say. George has probably told her what I said the other day about me wanting to be a boy. I've been waiting for this moment, waiting and fearing this moment for which I am still not ready.

"Alex, are you gay?"

I look at her.

"Again, you don't have to answer me if you don't want to. The only reason I ask you is because I can see you feel lost, and these issues in school . . . "

"School? Whaddya mean?

"Well, George told me you got into another fight."

I look at Amanda. She gives me a sweet, subtle smile. It's inviting me to open up, to share like that first day I met her.

"So, are you gay?"

I don't know what to say. I wish an easy answer would come to me, but it doesn't. "It's complicated. I . . . I don't see myself like a girl-girl. I . . . " I can't say anything else. I take a big breath and ask, "Has George told you what we talked about the other day?"

Amanda says no.

I cover my face and break down. I jump into her arms and cry. I say, "I talked to him about it, this same thing. Amanda, I don't know what to do."

Amanda holds me in her arms and caresses my back. She doesn't say anything. She just holds me there. I inhale, sit back in my chair and say, "I . . . I just don't wanna be a girl. I hate being a girl. I wish I was a boy."

Amanda's eyes open big, then she closes them. She exhales and takes my hands. There is so much love in her. I can feel it. I start crying again.

"I'm different, I know. But I'm the same. I'm Alex. I don't understand why people won't accept it," I tell her.

"First, Alex, you have to accept yourself. Have you accepted yourself?"

I shrug and say, "Kinda."

She stands up and starts combing my hair and looks at me through the mirror as she says, "I can't imagine what you feel. I guess no one can. I remember when George came out, it was beautiful and sad at the same time."

"Were you disappointed?"

"No, that's not what I mean. I would never be disappointed in George. I was sad because, how can I explain this? Sad because being *different* is hard. It's always hard. Being gay means you may have to face people that do not understand you, people who are willing to hurt you. You know what I mean?"

"Yes, I do."

"I was sad because I knew things would not be easy for George. The same with you, things won't be easy, but . . . you have to be true to yourself, Alex. It's very brave to say what you just did. I'm proud of you."

"Proud? Proud that I came out to you?"

"Proud that you came out to yourself." Amanda stands up. She caresses my cheek and cleans the tears off my eyes. Then she says, "Now, why don't we start working on your hair? What am I doing today?"

I shrug, frown.

"Would you let me do something a little bit crazy?"

"Like what?"

"I was thinking of making it shorter on the sides, leaving this out here and . . . " I can see Amanda studying my hair and deciding what to do with it. Then she offers, "How about coloring this small part of your hair? With bright blue. Whaddya think?"

"Blue? Are you serious?"

"Why not? Let's take the blue out of you and put it up here." Amanda pulls on a patch of my hair.

It does sound like a fantastic idea. "Let's do it!"

Amanda and I then talk about other stuff. I tell her about school and stupid Philip Carson. I tell her about Maggie and Jake. I tell her about me and Jake. I tell her how George has promised me a fantastic late-birthday present. Then she says, "Oh, I forgot to tell you. I met your Dad a few days ago. I was outside, smoking, and . . . He's quite the gentleman."

"You talked to him?"

"Yeah, we had a nice chat."

I smile. Wouldn't it be great? My dad and Amanda together? We could finally have a woman in the house, and George and I, we could be brothers. I turn to Amanda and say, "You know he's single, right? Single and available."

Amanda laughs and says, "Hold your horses. This gal is not on the market."

Amanda charges me only for the haircut, not the color. "Color is on the house," she says.

Amanda gives me a hug and we say goodbye. "I hope your brother gets better," she says.

Yeah, I hope Elliot gets better, too. I wish Dad had let me or Joe go with him to San Antonio, but he said no. He insisted that he needed us here. "Elliot is at the Brooke Army Medical Center, the best when it comes to burns." It's incredible. My brother hasn't even been sent to war and he's already injured.

I get home and see Joe is working in the barn. He tells me that he's just talked to Dad. "Elliot has second- and third-degree burns on his arms. He's stable, but they've drugged him for the pain . . ."

Joe then looks at me and makes a face. "What's this?" he says, pointing at my blue lock of hair.

"Blue hair. What else did Dad say?"

"He said, *Don't let Alex color her hair.*"

"Oh, shut up."

Joe smiles. He hands me the broom and asks me

to help him around the barn. I think of all the times we did this together—Joe, Elliot, and me. I decide that everything will be fine. My brother will be fine. He's going to get better, and before we know it he will be back with us.

As we're doing our chores, Joe's phone rings. He goes outside and talks. I can't hear everything he's saying except for, "Mia, tell me this isn't happening." It's the girl who called him the other day. I go out and try to ask him what is going on. He looks upset. He tells me to go finish the barn. He walks far from the barn. I can see him arguing or something. I go back to my work. When he comes back he says he has to leave.

"I'll be back later, okay? You finish this."

"Where are you going?"

"I'll be back later. You're in charge of dinner."

"But . . . but, what's going on? One of these days you'll have to explain me what is it that you . . . "

But Joe has walked away. He goes in the house and a minute later he is in his car driving away.

He always does this. He leaves when we are in the middle of something. Dad hates it when he does it.

Joe is an awful farmer. No. He's an awful boss. No. He is an awful man. Fine, I may be exaggerating, but the fact is that my brother Joe just left and there is still so much to do here. I mean, I can do it myself, of course, but it wouldn't hurt to have some help.

When it comes to the farm, Joe's super disorganized. Yesterday he had to deliver some product to Hilliard at nine in the morning, and, of course, he forgot. Tomorrow he has another couple of deliveries so I better finish this and start prepping everything ahead of time so he doesn't get all cranky.

When I'm done, I start working on tomorrow's deliveries. My phone rings,

"Hey, you," George says. "How could you come to my mom's and not stop by to say hello to me?"

"And hello to you, too," I say.

"Don't you love me anymore?" he asks in his most dramatic tone.

"Sorry, man, I had stuff to do on the farm. What's up? Or did you just call to preach to me?"

"I called to see if you are still up for tomorrow. Remember, Alex, I'm taking you to get your birthday present."

"Yeah, I'm in."

"Okay, perfect. Hey, you wanna come over later and watch TV or something?"

"I wish I could, but I got a ton of shit to do here."

"Come on, Alex. I'm bored to death."

"Why don't you come here? If you help me, I'll finish faster and then we can just hang out."

"Fine. Tell me again, how do I get to farmworld?"

When George arrives, he asks me to show him our farm. When he sees the fields, he sings, "Strawberry fields forevaaah." He checks everything out and keeps saying he can't believe someone could actually wanna be a farmer for life. As we are walking inside the house, we see Jake outside of his. George says, "Well, hello, Jake!" Jake just says, "Hey."

After we finish our work, we go directly to the

living room. George asks me for the remote and starts changing channels.

"You know, many girls in school drool for Jake. It's a shame Jake has the hots for you. This is so an episode of *Gossip Girl* or *Glee*."

"Shut up," I say as I go to the kitchen to get us some snacks.

"Oh, come on, you know he does. What do you wanna watch? *America's Next Top Model?*"

"Oh, yeah, it's my favorite," I say sarcastically.

"I forgot—you only watch football and shit."

"I like *The Walking Dead* and *Law and Order*, too. Everything I know about killing zombies or about the New York legal system, I've learned from them."

"Ha, ha. Hey, so what time tomorrow?"

"I dunno, whenever."

"I'm sorry I've been rain-checking on you, with the dance and everything."

"It's okay, George, no problem. And you know

you don't have to, right? I mean my birthday was weeks ago and. . . "

"Ten-ish it is."

George is taking me to Columbus. He says he has the perfect gift for me and it can only be purchased in a special store in Columbus. I tell him to get it by himself, but he says that he needs me to actually try it on before buying it. I'm worried he's thinking of buying me a fucking strap-on or something.

"Excellent. We'll have to stop by some beauty supply shops, too. Mom let me go under the condition that I bring her some shit for the salon."

"Sure, no problem. I only hope my brother doesn't make me go with him to do deliveries tomorrow," I mutter as I fix some sandwiches.

"Joe! He's so handsome."

"And so *hetero*."

"Have you given any thought to what we talked about the other day?"

"What?"

"Come on, you know. You wanting to be a man?" George yells.

"Shut up, someone might hear you," I say as I walk into the living room with our food.

"I thought you said no one's here?"

"I know, but . . . "

"Well, I think we must do some research and find out what you need to do to transition."

"Transition?"

"Yes, that's what you call it when you're a woman who wants to be a man or you are a man who wants to be a woman."

"Is that even possible?"

"Yup. You have a computer? Let me show you something."

"In my room."

"Okay, let's go then."

This is George's first time in my house and he moves around as if he has been coming here forever. He drags me upstairs. I take him to my room. Because of his reaction to the "decoration" of my room, I'm sure this will be the first and last time he comes. George has taken on the post of being my queer advisor or something. He sits down on my desk and Googles the word, *transgender*. I tell him I've heard the word before.

"Look. According to this, there are two types of transgendered people. MTF: male-to-female, and FTM: female-to-male, which is what you are. FTMs take testosterone and this hormone helps them thicken their skin and, believe it or not, grow hair on their face and chest," George says.

"Are you kidding? Is that even possible?" It's the answer to my dreams, a mustache and a beard, just like my dad. That would be so badass.

"From what I've read, it seems that in order to get started on a T-cocktail—T being testosterone, of course—you must go to therapy first. There are some clinics that . . . "

"Wait, wait. What?"

"If someone is seriously looking to transition,

they have to take testosterone. You do want to transition, right?"

I shrug and say, "I don't know . . . I really don't." I had never considered this. "It all sounds so incredible."

"Well, yeah, now you know it is not impossible. Watch this video of a Canadian kid who transitioned. It's amazing. He was in a girls' beauty pageant."

"What? And then she became a he?"

"Yup. Now wait. This is where we are going tomorrow." George types something else in Google, "I know it's supposed to be a surprise, but I can't help myself. I am dying for you to see it."

"What is this?" I ask George as I wander, amazed, through the web page and their products on sale. "How did you find out about this place?"

"A girl never reveals her secrets. You should know that from when you were actually a girl," George says as he clicks here and there. The name of the store is He, She, It, and in George's words, it's the queerest place in town. They sell clothes, accessories, and anything else you can imagine for the gay community.

"Isn't it incredible? Can you believe that this place is right in Columbus? Such a square-minded place has *this*. Here it is. See?" George shows me what seems to be a tank top.

"What is that?"

"This, my dear Alexander, is a binder."

Alexander, I like the sound of it. Alexander. That's me. "A binder? What the fuck is that?" I say as I look at it.

"Let me illuminate you with my wisdom." George clicks on a picture and I see two pictures of a girl. In one of them she is wearing a bra, in the other one, though, she is wearing that thing, and her boobs have sorta disappeared.

"Are you serious? That thing actually works?"

"Yup. It's a must for all women who want to be men. I guess it's also a must for chubby guys with boobs."

"Wow. Can I order it online, then?"

"No, Alexander. That's why we must go to Columbus tomorrow. You need to try it on first to make sure we have your size."

George and I spend the rest of the time fooling around with my computer. When he leaves, I realize it's late and I haven't made dinner for me and Joe. I text him and ask him what is he in the mood for, but he doesn't reply. "Tuna casserole it is," I tell myself.

I end up eating on my own. Joe texts me saying he will be home later than he expected. I clean the kitchen, take a shower, and go to bed. I'm excited, very excited about tomorrow. George is making a man out of me.

* * *

This tall, skinny guy with a retro-looking suit, bowtie, and a bobbed blue wig greets us. "Welcome, have you been here before?"

George and I shake our heads and say, "No."

He smiles and says, "Well, let me show you around." As we walk through the aisles, he asks, "Are you guys looking for anything in particular?"

"Yes," George says. "We're looking for a binder for my friend."

The guy looks at me and says, "This way."

Tall-skinny-wigged guy shows us the binder section and helps us find a size for me; he chooses a couple of binders and walks us to the dressing room. He opens a curtain for us and we walk in to what looks like a diva's dressing room. It has mirrors on three walls, and a vintage gold dressing chair in the corner. "Take your time."

He leaves and I tell George, "I can't put this on. What if someone sees me?"

"Come on, don't be silly. This is why we came all the way here. Here, hold this." George gives me his messenger bag and he picks up a binder. "This one's my size. I'll try it on so you can see it's no biggie, then you try it on."

George starts taking off his layers. When he pulls

his t-shirt over his head, I get a look at his smooth chest. No hair! I wonder if he doesn't have any or if he shaves or waxes or something? George is pretty fit for someone who doesn't go to the gym or play any sports.

He puts on the tank and I can see how it adjusts perfectly to his body, all tight. "See?" Well, I don't have boobs whatsoever, but see how the spandex pulls my skin? This is what you can use to hide the girls." George checks himself out in all three mirrors.

"The girls?" I wondered aloud. I am such an idiot.

"Your boobs, Alexander, your boobs. Here, you try the one I gave you. I'm sure that's your size." I start to pull my top off and realize that I don't feel comfortable doing it in front of him.

"Eh, do you think you could step out for a minute?"

"Are you serious? But we're all girls here."

"Just get the hell out, George," I growl at him.

"Fine."

I take off all my clothes and take a minute to examine my body, I see my "girls." I hate them. They're not too big, thankfully, but they make my body look wrong. I cover my nipples with my hands and I push them into my chest while looking at myself in the mirrors. How I wish they weren't there. I picture myself with George's chest.

"You ready, Alexander?"

"Hold on." I put on the binder. It is not that easy to push my head through it. I pull the binder all the way down to my waist. I feel how my body constricts inside it. I look at myself in the mirror again. I know "the girls" are there, but they are not all there. "Okay!" I say to George.

"Wow. How do you feel?"

"Weird but great."

"Should we check out some other styles and colors? I believe we need to get a beige one and a black one—just like buying bras."

I don't even pay attention to what George is

saying. I can't take my eyes off of the reflection in the mirror. I touch my chest; it feels awesome.

"Do you think we can get something tighter than this?" I ask George.

"Well, we don't want to constrict your breathing, but I'm sure we can find something else."

I try on a few more. Just for laughs, George makes me try on some of the other clothes they sell in this store. I ask him why the store is called He, She, It. I mean, I get they sell stuff for girls who wanna be boys and boys who wanna be girls, but what is the "It" part of all this?

"The sex toys, of course."

"Sex toys, are you serious?"

"Yup, you interested? Maybe you can get a plastic penis."

"Aaghh, no thank you very much," I protest.

"There are plastic penises that women wear so they can pee like men."

"Seriously?"

"Yup. That's what Google says. Want me to ask?"

"No, no. Not this time," I say.

George buys me a binder as a present and I get myself a second one. Before we leave, I go to the bathroom and put one on.

* * *

"Do you think it's very expensive? You know, testosterone?" I ask George as we sit down to eat burgers.

"No clue, but that's why God invented smartphones. Here, Google it." As George hands me his phone, mine starts to ring. It's Dad.

"Hey Dad, how are things in San Antonio? How's . . . ?" I didn't even get to finish my sentence. It's Elliot's voice on the other end.

"Hey, Alex. Miss me?"

"Elliot, oh my God. How are you?" I wave my hands at George to tell him that it is my brother who is on the phone. "How do you feel? When are you coming home?"

"Well, everything hurts like hell, but I'm better.

I'm lucky, if there had been more third-degree burns, I wouldn't be talking to you right now. So, Dad is taking me home soon. I'll be on medical leave during my recovery."

"That's great!"

As I hang up the phone, I sigh, "My brother is going to be out of the hospital soon."

George looks at me. I see him glance at my chest before he says, "That's great news. Another man out," George says, smiling.

CHAPTER EIGHT
breasts

MONDAYS SUCK—EVERYBODY KNOWS THAT. ON Mondays, I normally hit snooze every five minutes. Not today. Not *this* Monday. I'm a new Alex with a new hairdo and my binder. I woke up earlier than usual just to get ready. Even Joe is surprised to see me up. He's on his way to work, he took some days off to work on the farm while Dad is away, but today he has to go back.

"Here's a twenty. Buy fried chicken or something at the supermarket. There's no way I'm eating tuna casserole for dinner again," he says.

"How about burgers?" I tell him. He shrugs. "Sure, anything but tuna, please." We bump into each other on his way out of the kitchen. He looks at me, then looks at my chest. I can see he notices something *different* about me. His eyes go from my chest to my hair and vice versa. I wonder if he will actually ask me something. "Okay, gotta go. See you tonight," he says before leaving.

First period starts at eight fifty a.m., and it's not even eight a.m. yet. I have the perfect amount of time to make myself a decent breakfast. Decent breakfast means instant oatmeal and toast. I'm about to start eating when someone knocks at the door. Jake, maybe? I run to open. No, it's not Jake.

A beautiful girl with long black hair stands in front of me, a girl I have never seen before. "Hi," she says. "I'm looking for Joe." I can't remember the last time someone came looking for my brother.

"Joe? You just missed him. He went to work." She opens her eyes big and wide and says, "Really? I thought he was only working on the farm these days." She turns her back and I see another girl, waiting in a car. The girl in front of me yells to the other one, "He's not here." It is now that I notice how skinny she is, except for a a bit of a belly.

The girl in the car asks, "So, Mia, whaddya wanna do?" Mia. I've heard that name.

"I should have called before coming. When will he be back?"

"Around five, I guess." She looks disappointed at my answer.

The girl in the car yells again, "Mia if he's not here, then let's go."

"Go where? I can't go back home, you know how Dad is." Mia looks worried, it seems she's about to cry.

I ask her, "Are you okay? Is there anything I can—"

"You're Alex, right?"

"Yes."

"Alex, I know this is going to sound super weird but, well . . . My dad, my dad sorta kicked me out. I have no place to go. That's my stepsister. I convinced her to drive me here, but she has to go now and . . . "

Mia, where have I heard this name? Before I can continue putting the dots together. Her belly. Her big belly.

Mia starts crying, "You know what? Forget it. Can you tell Joe that Mia was here and . . . "

"Are you . . . Are you guys . . . ? Are you guys, like, together?"

"Yes."

"And . . . ?" I point at her belly. "Are you . . . *pregnant?*"

"Yes."

"Does Joe know?"

"He does, and we were going to talk to my dad about it, but, well, Joe wanted to wait until your father got back, to talk to him first but, well . . . my dad found out and . . . "

Mia's stepsister comes out of the car and says, "So, are you staying or what? We can always try your Grandma."

Mia covers her face and says, "If dad didn't kill me, grandma definitely will."

Without thinking too much about it, I say, "Stay here."

Mia looks at me with her big eyes and says, "What?"

"Stay. Just stay. I mean, no one's going to kill you here. And you'll be alone. I'm on my way to school and Dad is out of town so . . . "

Mia's stepsister, who is now standing right behind Mia, cuts in. "Smart idea, that way when Joe gets home you guys can talk."

Mia shakes her head. "Are you crazy? I can't . . . "

I interrupt her, "Why not? That's why you came for, right?" I point at the small suitcase sitting next to her. "Come on, it will be just fine. I was about to have breakfast, have you guys eaten?"

Mia's stepsister smiles at me and says, "It seems you're in good hands here, Mia. Stay. I will call you once Dad is—"

"Not crazy?" Mia finishes.

"I was going to say not as mad as he is now, but . . . "

They hug each other before waving goodbye.

I invite her inside the house and lead her to the kitchen. I look at her from behind: she seems like a regular skinny girl. But, when she turns around—booom, her tummy goes pop. Oh, and a pair of huge boobs. I'm not good at this, but I'm guessing she's at least four or five months pregnant.

She says no to my instant oatmeal, but she accepts toast. I show her around the house—living room, TV, remote, bathroom. I can see she's nervous.

I am not looking forward to what's going to happen when Joe comes back. Mia seems nice and sweet; I can't picture her with my brother. I'm afraid Joe is going to kick my ass. But what am I supposed to do? It's cold outside, and it sounded like she had no place to go.

Mia tells me she has been dating my brother for almost a year. *A whole year.* It was an on-and-off thing. Then she got pregnant, and Joe told her he would make it all good for them.

She's not so surprised that Joe never told us about her.

"Your brother is weird, isn't he? You know, I've never met any of his friends."

"That's because he doesn't have all that many. Joe is kind of a hermit. His best friend is that car," I tell her.

Mia smiles.

"Okay, gotta go to school now. Please help yourself. I'll be back around four."

Mia looks at me. I see her eyes becoming glassy. "Thank you. Thank you so much."

* * *

School goes fine. No one seems to notice something different in me, except for Maggie. Her locker is right across from mine and when she notices my chest, she looks at me all weird, and I say, "Hey

Maggie, what's up?" And I walk away; I don't even give her a chance to say anything. Before going to class I go to the restroom. I wanna see myself in the mirror one more time, but it's crowded by girls who are doing their makeup and shit. Then it hits me, if I actually do what George says and start transitioning, I would also have to start using the men's restroom. Maybe I can even get that peeing penis. Would I be able to do that?

* * *

It's almost six and my brother hasn't showed up yet. I thank Mia for dinner. I forgot to buy food and she cooked for us. Tomato soup and chicken fried steak. Delicious. I start picking up the plates, but she stops me.

"Let me, I'll do it. I don't mind."

"Let's do it together," I say.

"Alex, do you think your father will let me stay

here? I can't go back to my family. I just can't. Dad wants me to give away the baby."

Fuck. What'd you say to that? Mia seems lost and desperate. I walk to her side, hold her hands in mine, and tell her not to worry.

"My brother will solve all this, you'll see. And Dad, you shouldn't worry about him—he's got this big, fat heart. He'll be shocked and will yell a little at first, but I'm sure he'll be delighted to be a grandpa."

"I wish I had a brother like you, Alex," Mia says, giving me a hug.

What? Mia thinks I am a boy? How's that even possible? I know I have to tell her something, I know I should explain, but I wanna savor this moment.

"Alex? Alex, where are you?" Joe is home. He walks in with groceries and I meet him halfway.

"Here, let me help," I say.

"No, just get what I left in the car. Hey, it smells good in here. You might make a good lady of the house after all . . . " Joe puts the groceries on the counter, then he sees Mia.

"Mia? What are . . . how did you . . .?" Joe turns, looks at me.

I can tell he has a million questions going through his head, but he doesn't say anything. It's like Mia's eyes and face tell him all. He wraps his arms around her. Mia cries on his shoulder.

"My dad found out. He went crazy and kicked me out. I had no place to go."

"I'm so sorry. I should've . . . I don't know why I told you to wait. You stay here, with me, with us. We'll work things out." Mia and Joe hug each other and start whispering *I-love-you*'s. I decide to leave them to it.

I hear Mia saying, "You must be hungry. Come, I made dinner."

Finally, a real woman is in our house.

* * *

Joe sets Mia up in his room. I hear them talking, then they come into the TV room downstairs,

"Alex, I'm so sorry I thought you were a boy. I got confused, I . . . Joe always say Alex this, Alex that, but he never said Alex was a—I mean—is my sister and not my brother." Mia fumbles with the words.

Joe walks behind her. "I told her everyone confuses you for a boy," he says. "Alex is used to it by now. I mean, look at her." Joe points at my hair and the flannel shirt I'm wearing. I can tell he's staring again at my chest, but this time he goes and asks, "Hey, where are your boobs?"

I don't reply.

"Joe!" Mia says in a shocked tone. "She's your baby sister."

"Ha! Alex has never been a baby sister."

I'm aware that bringing this up is not the best idea right now, but I decide to do it anyway. "Actually . . . " I take a long pause to control my fear, and finally say, "Actually I am transitioning."

"Transitioning? What the fuck is that?" Joe looks dumbfounded. He lets go of Mia's hand and orders me to stand up. Mia stares at me, trying to understand what's happening.

"What's going on, Alexandra? What did you do?" He's pointing at my breasts.

His hands are too close, so I push them away. "Nothing, I didn't do anything. It's just that, Joe, you'd better sit down for this."

Joe ignores me and says, "What the fuck is going on, Alexandra? Tell me." I sit down on the sofa and Mia does the same. Her eyes dart from Joe to me and then back to Joe. Finally, he sits down.

"First of all, stop calling me, Alexandra. My name is Alex, just Alex." Then I unbutton my shirt and show him the binder, "See? Here are my breasts, but I'm hiding them with this thing because, because . . . because I am transitioning."

"Again with that fucking word," Joe says. "What the fuck does that even mean?"

Mia intervenes. "If I'm right, I believe that what Alex is trying to say is that she wants to be a boy. She's transitioning from female to male. Am I right, Alex?"

I nod. Mia and I both look at Joe who seems to be lost in some other galaxy.

"What? You whaaat? Alex, you're a lesbian, aren't you? That's what we all think, you know—Dad, Elliot, and me. We just never talk about it."

"No. I am not a lesbian. I am a man. I wanna be a man. I know it's hard to understand, but I have always, always, always felt like a boy inside, and . . . well, I never dared to do something about it. I didn't even know I was transsexual."

"Trans-*what*? I'm getting a headache, Alex. Are you serious? What am I going to tell Dad? He leaves me in charge and he will come back to find out that he's a grandfather-to-be and that his daughter is turning into a *transi, transte* . . . "

"Transsexual, Joe," Mia adds.

"I don't understand a thing," says Joe.

Mia explains, "Alex is a girl on the outside, but she feels like a man on the inside."

Joe lets out a breath like a tire going flat. "God, why? How? This is too much for one day," he says.

"I'm going to bed. We'll talk about this tomorrow, it's too much for one day."

He stands up and asks Mia if she's coming. "I'll be up in a minute," she says. "I think Alex and I need to chat about girl/boy stuff now."

Joe leaves the room. Mia moves closer to me, and a look of pain passes over her face. "Oh my God, these hurt." She hugs her breasts.

"What does it feel like to be pregnant?" I ask her.

Mia pauses before saying, "Honestly? It sucks. Really. I pee all the time. I feel heavy. And my breasts—God, my breasts hurt all the time." Mia looks at me then asks, "How 'bout yours? Do they hurt under that thing?"

"A little bit, yeah. But I feel great."

CHAPTER NINE
what are you?

"ALEX, YOU WILL BE IN DETENTION FOR TWO WEEKS. If this doesn't teach you a lesson, I don't know what will," Vice Principal Harris says. "Also, you will be seeing Mrs. Smith once a week until the end of the semester." Mrs. Smith looks at me and smiles.

"What about Carson—is he getting detention *and* counseling, too?" I realize that I sound like a child, so I change my tone before adding, "I mean, I know that I crossed a line, but—"

"Whatever we decide to do with Philip Carson is none of your business and you know it," he says.

"But Philip—" I try to make an argument, but

the counselor interrupts me, "Mr. Carson is still with the nurse. You hit him very hard. He's in really bad shape. Let's hope his parents don't decide to pursue further action."

"Action? What does that even mean?" I yell. I am so pissed off that I'm not sure if I am really yelling, but Mrs. Smith's voice sounds more like a whisper compared to mine.

"Alex," she says, "Carson's parents could file a complaint. They could even press charges."

"And?"

The vice principal leans forward and gives me this big fake smile he uses before giving you bad news, "And, Alex, if charges are pressed we are talking about community service or even juvenile detention."

I can't believe what I'm hearing. Phillip Carson bullies everyone at school. Philip Carson is the one who started this whole thing with me. He's the one who started with the name-calling and pushing me around, but *I* am the one who might end up in deep shit. "You're kidding. You can't do that to me."

"We might have to before you become a danger to other students," he warns.

A danger? I still don't understand. Phillip Carson is the bully.

What happened was, we were in the gym. Mr. Wood decided to have a girls against boys challenge activity, like it's the 1950s or something. I was already in a bad mood, because now that I am learning more about who I am on the inside, and started using my binder, I feel like I really don't belong anywhere. Which is my team, girls or boys?

I haven't really talked to anyone about my transitioning except for Joe, Mia, and, of course, George. I am trying to do it slowly. George calls me Alexander all the time and refers to me as *he* when talking to other people about me. I don't like it when he does it in school, though. I told him I wasn't ready to take such a big step. I've also stopped using the girls' bathroom at school. Not that I am using the boys', I am just not using any of them. It has been a huge challenge because I normally have to pee a couple of times a day. Now I have to restrict my water intake or my bladder will explode.

I don't want to use the girls' bathroom, but I can't use the boys' bathroom because I might get in trouble. Same goes for the locker room. So, these last couple of weeks, I've had to put my normal clothes over my sweaty gym clothes after PE class.

When Mr. Wood said, "Make two groups, girls and boys, and choose a leader for your group," I obviously wanted to be with the boys, but I knew I couldn't. Really, I didn't have any decision to make. I just had walk over to my team, but instead, I stood there like an idiot.

"Miss Jenkins," The coach yelled at me. "Why aren't you moving?"

Before I could answer, stupid asshole Philip Carson said, "Miss Jenkins actually doesn't know which is her group. *She* is a *he*, or *he* is a *she*, however you want." Everyone started laughing.

"No one asked your opinion, Carson," the coach said before addressing me. "Miss Jenkins, let's go."

I started walking to my team when Philip said, "Wait, that's not fair. You said all girls and all boys. Jenkins should be with us. Can't you tell that she is a boy? No wait, you're right, he is a girl. Wait no. Jenkins, WHAT ARE YOU?"

My whole life I've been mistaken for a boy and it has always been a sort of validation of the inner me. But Philip Carson was trying to humiliate me.

"Mr. Carson! Enough! I will not tolerate—"

"Why do you keep trying to look like a dude, Jenkins? You are not a man," Philip added.

"And neither are you, Carson." I blindsided him, knocking him down, only this time he got up right away and punched me back. I did lose my balance a bit, but I stood my ground. I gave him a shot to the stomach and as he bent over, I hit him in the back. He was back on the floor.

"Fucking dyke!" he cried. Mr. Wood and some of the guys tried to stop me, but I was so fucking angry that they couldn't hold me back. I managed to get loose, and straddle Philip Carson. I kept pounding him hard in the face.

"Don't you dare call me a dyke again! I'm not a dyke!" I yelled.

It felt like an eternity, but the whole thing happened in less than a minute. Mr. Wood and some of the guys pulled me off. The girls surrounded Philip and helped him up as they gasped at his face.

"Quick, someone take him to the nurse. Jenkins, you come with me to the office. The rest of you, hit the showers."

Mr. Wood pulled me by the arm and walked me all the way to the main office.

I was still pissed and said, "I can walk on my own," a couple of times, but he didn't wanna hear it.

"Shut up, Miss Jenkins. Just keep your mouth shut," he repeated.

This is my fourth time in this office since the

semester started. Things don't look good. At least Dad isn't back from San Antonio.

* * *

"Are you okay, Alex?" Jake asks. His locker is right next to mine. I slam the door of my locker and look at him. I want to be an ass and say, *Oh, you are talking to me now?*, but he looks genuinely worried.

"As okay as I can be, considering I have to stay for detention forever and have counseling for the rest of my high school life."

"Are you serious?" he says.

"No. Detention won't last forever and counseling won't be the rest of my life, but it's going to feel like it. Who told you?" I put on my backpack. It is the last period so after this I have to go to the detention room.

"Your BFF."

BFF? Jake is trying to make me laugh. He would never say BFF, LOL or any of those stupid text acronyms. But he notices that it doesn't work, so he goes back to normal human talk, "I mean, George. He told me Philip Carson pushed you too far and you fucked him up pretty bad."

"Yup, that's exactly what happened."

"Alex, you need to be careful. Philip and his friends are fucking assholes and . . . I don't know . . . after this, I can see him trying to get you back."

"I'll be fine, don't worry. I gotta go."

"Alex, wait. I am serious, be careful."

"Okay."

"Promise?"

"Promise." I start to head off when Jake says, "Hey, what time will you get out of detention?"

"Six, I think. Why?"

"Well, I can wait for you. So you don't go home alone. It's gonna be dark when you leave."

"Are you crazy? I don't want you to stay here after school. Don't worry."

"I do worry. What if you kill somebody?" He gives me a smile, and I can tell that Jake and I are back to being buddies. "Listen, how about I come back and we ride home together?"

I don't know what has gotten into Jake. First he tells me he loves me, then he tells me to piss off, and now . . .

"No Jake, there's no need. I'll be fine. Even if Philip tries to do something, I can handle him without killing him."

"Okay," but before leaving, he adds, "Alex, you and I need to talk—you know that, don't you?"

"Yeah. Later today, maybe?"

Jake nods in agreement and we part ways. It was actually nice to see that he was so concerned. He has always been my best friend. I hope we can work things out and go back to being friends.

* * *

I hate detention. There's really nothing you can do but fix your eyes on the blackboard. Some of the kids do their homework, but I don't. I usually sit there and daydream about jeeps or beards or whatever. There are two freshmen there with me. These guys were caught smoking in the bathroom. They look like total stoner burnouts.

I grabbed a book before getting here to try and make the time go by faster. It's a novel that George lent me the other day called, *Sunny*. The story is about Michael, a kid who feels he should have been born a girl. When everyone is sleeping at night, he puts on his older sister's dresses and makeup. It makes me smile because I would wear my brothers' clothes, too, only I didn't have to hide to do it. I didn't know I wasn't supposed to, and no one thought it was strange. Everyone—Dad, Elliot, and Joe—pretty much let me be. Until I had my first period and my body started turning into something I couldn't identify with.

I was in middle school and we were in PE. It's seems like the worst moments of my life have happened during PE. Anyway, I had been feeling weird that day but didn't pay much attention to it. So, there I was running around when all of a sudden I feel something warm running down my legs, like I had peed my pants. I stopped dead in my tracks, and sat down to find a huge dark spot on my shorts.

I wasn't stupid; I knew what it was. I ran out of the gym and straight to the office to ask for the phone. For a second I thought about calling Dad, but I was embarrassed, and I dialed Jake's mom instead. "Debbie, it's Alex. Can you pick me up, I . . . I don't feel well. I need you. I . . . ," I whispered so no one else would know, "I got my period."

Debbie came right away, signed me out of school for the day and took me with her. As soon as we got in her car she said, "Oh, Alex, aren't you excited? I know this sucks, but you aren't a kid anymore. You're a woman now. Remember we talked about this?" She drove me to the pharmacy to buy supplies for my *ladyness*.

Before she dropped me off at home, I told her,

"I don't want this. I don't wanna be a woman. I wanna be a kid." I didn't know exactly what I was trying to say, but looking back on it now, I think I knew right then that I wanted to remain a kid, just bigger. I don't mean a big kid, but the person I was as a child in an adult body, and not change into someone who can have babies. Getting my period screwed my life in so many ways. It made me a girl, and it made me hate being a girl even more.

Just like Sunny, the character in the novel, I have always known that I was born in the wrong body. In the novel, Sunny talks to the principal and tries to convince everyone in school to refer to him as a *she*. "No more Michael, my name is Sunny," he says.

I want to do the same. I want to tell everyone to see me as a *he*. No one calls me Alexandra anyway, so it shouldn't be that difficult. But becoming a man will require more than just changing my name or pronoun. I wonder how hard it is to get started on testosterone. I read that once you're taking testosterone your period stops. That would be great, no more girl-blood every month.

* * *

It's only six p.m. and it *is* already dark. The other two detention kids left already. I'm the only one outside the school. I take the lock of my bike and get on. George texts me. He wants me to go his place, but I'm really hungry. All I want is to go home.

Mia has been with us a week, and she's been feeding us like pigs. I like her cooking; she says she dreams about having small dinner parties. I like her being a part of the family. This morning she asked me, "How do you want your eggs, over easy or sunny-side up?" Maybe this is normal for everyone else in the world, but at home the question was always, "Do you want eggs or not?" Now I even get to choose.

But Mia is more than just a cook; she's a great

woman. Last night we talked for hours. She was telling me how a friend of a friend was just like me. She was uncomfortable with her body and her life. "She is transitioning, just like you." This girl, well, this boy is twenty-one and just started taking hormone therapy.

Really, Mia is turning out to be the best thing that could have happened to us. Joe hasn't told Dad the whole story. He did say that his girlfriend is living with us because her family kicked her out, but he failed to mention that Mia is having his baby. Dad is still in San Antonio with Elliot. I told Joe there's no way Dad won't accept Mia, considering her whole family situation, but I guess he's afraid of what Dad will say. He's always been a bit of a chicken.

Joe says I have to wait to talk to Dad about my transitioning. He says that Dad will reject the whole idea. "What about you?" I asked Joe. "Do you still reject my being a boy?"

He did not say anything at first, but he looked

at me and said, "I guess not . . . I just want you to be happy."

I'm starving. I wonder what Mia made for dinner. There's a car behind me, it hasn't passed. Why doesn't he just pass? I hate how people don't get that cyclists have a right to use a full lane. "Man, just get over it. This is my lane. If you wanna go, just pass already!"

Then the car goes to pass and I see that it's Philip Carson driving. What is he doing? Fuck. Fuck. Fuck. This doesn't look good.

He cuts me off with the car and I almost crash into him. Asshole. I'm so mad that I leave my bike on the road and run to the car to yell at him, "What the fuck, Philip? Can't you drive like a normal person?"

Then I hear them; Philip's friends get out of the car. There are three of them here. One of them says, "Normal? You talkin' about being a normal person?" I don't know his name, but he's in Philip's pack of dogs. They all begin laughing, and I feel a little nervous.

As usual, my mouth starts talking before my brain does any thinking. "Wow, you have bodyguards now, Philip? What is it, you afraid of me?" Big mouth.

"Afraid of you? Afraid of a little pussy like you? Come on, Alexandra."

"Don't call me that."

"Don't call you what, pussy or Alexandra?"

"Fucking asshole, I'm not going to waste my time with you," I say as I try to get back to my bike. But one of Philip's friends already has it.

"Your bike? You want your bike?" He holds it in the air and throws it in the ditch to the side of the road. I run straight at the guy, knocking him over.

When he's on the ground, I try to go for my bike, but the other guy grabs me by the arm. "Oh no, you don't. You're ours now."

"Let me go, you motherfucker, let me go."

"Wow, Lady Dyke has a dirty mouth," the guy says, then turns to Philip and asks, "What do you want to do?"

"Get her in the car, let's go before someone sees us."

I struggle to get away, but they are too strong. I yell as loud as I can, "No! Leave me alone! Let me go, let me go!"

"You're coming with us. I'm going to get you once and for all. I'm tired of your bitching."

I try to calm myself down, but I can't, I just can't. "Tired of my bitching or tired of me kicking your ass, Philip?" I say to cover how scared I am.

Philip turns red and then he punches me in the stomach. "Shut the fuck up," he says.

My phone starts ringing, but one of the guys takes it from my pocket and says, "Look, your girl is calling her."

"Who?"

"Maggie. Look." The guy says as he holds my phone up. "What do you want me to do?" the guy says. Philip takes my phone out of his friend's hand and throws it away.

"What's up with you and Maggie, you lesbo? Why is she defending you all the time?"

"Because she's my friend," I tell him. "And she likes me more than she will ever like you, you—" I don't even get to finish my sentence. Philip punches me in the stomach again.

"Let's go," he tells his friends.

I'm shoved inside the car. They sit with me in the backseat. Philip gets in the front seat and drives away. We pass houses, we pass farms, we pass my farm and Jake's, and as the road starts getting darker I get more scared of what they have planned for me.

The lake, we are driving to the lake. My lake.

Philip parks near the campground, then he asks his friends to pull me out. Those assholes call me names and push me around. They open my shirt; they wanna know how I hid my boobs. They rip my binder off. I cover myself but they keep pulling my arms, "See you are a girl, not a fucking boy," one of them says.

"Her boobs are small," someone else points out.

"Are they? Let's look again," says Philip.

"Leave me alone!" I yell, but they ignore me. "You motherfuckers!" My words make them so mad that they take turns kicking me in the chest.

I try to stand up, but Philip pushes me to the ground, and then gets on top of me. He stares at me and says, "If you didn't try so hard to look like a man you might actually be pretty." Then he licks my face, before punching me with all his strength.

A sinking dread fills my stomach. I know what he's up to, I just know it. "Stop, stop, please," I yell as he pulls down my pants. "Don't . . . " I try to cover myself.

He tries to stick his hand inside of me first, and then he notices it. I am bleeding. He cleans his hand on the ground and says, "Argh, she's fucking bleeding. Bitch is on her fucking period."

His friends go, "That's sick."

"She's dirty, leave her."

Then Philip looks at me and says, "You see? If

you're bleeding, that means you are a girl. A girl!" He's kicking me again and again as he says, "A girl! You understand? You are a girl, you weirdo! Can't go against nature."

One kick after another. I close my eyes. I feel weak. I'm gonna pass out. Then, one of his friends stops him. "Stop it, Philip. You're gonna kill her, stop it."

Philip finally stops. In my half-conscious state, I feel him right next to me. I hear him growl in my ear, "Let that be a lesson to you, you fucking dyke. I'm a real man, not like you and your faggot friends."

While I lay there, gagging on the blood from my shattered face, I feel a warm stream of liquid pouring over my head. He's laughing as he pisses on me.

"Let's go, Philip." His friends seem anxious to get out of here.

"Give me a second," he replies as he zips up the fly of his pants. "You better not say a word about this to anyone or we'll do it again." He kicks me one last time, and then I hear them walk back to the car and drive away.

My body is screaming in pain. *I have to go*, I tell myself. I try to get up and limp my way home. But I can't, I just can't. I close my eyes.

I am here, all alone at the lake.

My lake.

* * *

I don't know how long it's been. The sound of their voices wakes me up.

"Alex? Oh my God, Alex! Are you okay? Jake, Alex is here!" It's Maggie. She tries to pull me up but she can't.

"What happened to you, Alex?" Jake says as he joins Maggie. They help me up. They were both riding their bikes.

"Call your Mom, Jake." Maggie says.

"No, I'm calling her brother, and I am calling the police, too."

"How . . . how did you know . . . how did you know I was here?" I ask them.

"I saw you arguing with Phillip on the side of the road. I yelled at you, but you didn't hear me. Then I tried to call you, but you never answered. I ran, I ran to help you, but then they got you in the car," explains Maggie, crying. "I'm so stupid. I should have called the police right away . . ."

Jake covers me with his jacket and Maggie cleans my face with her shirt. I feel safe.

* * *

I should have gone to George's like he wanted me to, or accepted Jake's offer to come back for me after detention. Nothing would have happened, and I would not be in this bed, in this hospital, remembering over and over again what Philip and his friends did.

I can't move very much, but it doesn't matter because I feel like shit and all I wanna do is sleep and forget what happened. Everything keeps playing over and over again in my head. I try to think of other things, but my mind always goes back to that night. Sometimes I hear fragments of the things they said, or taste the blood and urine in mouth. Why can't the doctor give me something strong to take my pain away and put me to sleep? That's all I wanna do—sleep.

George came to visit after school. Maggie and Jake came too. I pretended to be sleeping. I didn't wanna talk to any of them. I could hear Jake and Maggie whispering to each other. I heard Jake saying, "Fucking Philip Carson. I'm gonna kill him."

Maggie calmed him down. "Stop it, Jake. We don't know for sure. I only saw them arguing on the side of the road. We can't do anything until she wakes up and talks to the police. Who knows what really happened out there?"

"Look at her, Maggie—this is what happened

to her. Oh, that's right, I forgot that you're now friends with Philip Carson."

Maggie simply said, "No, he's not my friend. He happens to be around me and my friends all the fucking time, but believe me he's far from being my friend. And if it turns out he did this to Alex, he will be sorry."

They stayed with me for a while. Then both of them kissed me and left.

Debbie spent the first night with me, holding my hand, caressing my arm. I could hear her weeping. From what I've heard, Amanda will stay tonight. I haven't been left alone since I arrived. Mia and Joe try to comfort me; they come and go. They encourage me to talk, but I don't want to. I don't wanna do anything at all, other than forget what happened.

* * *

The police are here now. They keep asking me

questions. The only thing I say is that three men attacked me. I say it was dark and couldn't see them. They want details. They ask about them, about their car. I say nothing. "I couldn't see," I repeat.

One of the officers tells Joe that they won't be able to do anything unless I identify them.

"Have you seen the work those fuckers did on my sister? Get those guys. Just fucking get them," Joe says.

One of the police officers tries to apologize.

"Please, just go," my brother says.

I'm afraid of how my dad will react when he learns what they did to me. I'm tired, everything hurts. I just wanna close my eyes and sleep.

"Hey, sweetie. Are you awake?" Amanda asks.

"Look, I got you this cream for your face. It should help with the healing." She sits down next to me and opens a jar.

"Does it look really bad?" I ask. Amanda can't help but smile.

"You see, you are worried about your looks even if you try to deny it," she says to make me smile. Carefully she puts some cream on my cheeks and my forehead. She moves her fingers as softly as she can. Her gentle caress feels nice on my skin.

"Oh, Alex, don't cry. It will all be okay. You will be okay. We're all here for you. We'll take care of you."

"Amanda," I say. "This is all my fault for trying to be someone I'm not. For being so impulsive, for being such a—"

"No, baby, this isn't your fault. You can't blame yourself."

"That's what Dad is going to say—that it's my fault. I know him."

"Your Dad will be happy to see that you are alive. He will be glad that you were strong enough to survive this."

* * *

Amanda was right. Dad didn't blame me for what happened. He's been sitting next to my bed since I was released from the hospital. He has brought me tea and cookies. He swears that no one will ever touch me again.

I say, "How do you know?"

Dad takes my hand and says, "I won't let anyone hurt you."

I say, "You can't keep people from hating me for the way I am."

He says, "No one hates you for the way you are. People fear what they don't understand. When people are afraid, they do stupid things. I'm sorry this happened, but I want you to stop thinking this was your fault. It wasn't."

Dad kisses my forehead. He looks at me and smiles, "You have your mother's eyes and your mother's strength . . . "

I look at Dad and ask him, "Why don't you ever talk about her? Why don't you share her with us?"

Dad's smile disapears from his face. "What do you mean?" he asks me.

"I dunno, I . . . I feel like you keep her for yourself."

Dad doesn't know what to say. He looks at me, then he looks around my room, and simply says, "I—that's not what . . . I'm sorry, Alex. I guess, I have. It's hard, you know? To talk about her. I promise you that when you get better, you and I will talk as much as you want. Now, you rest. We'll get through this, you'll see." My dad stands up and someone knocks on my door. "There's someone here to see you," he says. Elliot walks in, he's limping; he's got bandages on both his arms, and a sad face.

"Hey, you," he says. Dad leaves.

Elliot finds a place right next to me on my bed.

"How are you?" I ask him.

"I feel like shit," he says. "I smell like barbeque. Here, check it out." He places his hand on my nose. We both laugh. "How about you?" Elliot says, "How do *you* feel?"

"Better. I think."

"Hey, so Joe says there's something we need to talk about, you and I. Wanna tell me what it is?" I guess this is my chance. I could open up to him. I could explain to him about transitioning. If I tell him, then talking to Dad might be easier.

But, now I don't know if I want to. Not after what happened. Tears roll from my eyes. I take a sip of my tea and say, "Not now, Elliot, okay?"

"Fine, but you know you can tell me anything— *anything*—right, Alex?"

"Yeah. But now . . . I just wanna sleep."

"Oh, sure. I'm sorry, you must be tired." Elliot blows a kiss at me and leaves.

My ribs hurt, my nose hurts. Pain, all I feel is pain. I put on my headphones, turn on my iPod, and listen to Lorde's "White Teeth Teens." I turn off my lamp.

* * *

It's been more than a month since it happened. Christmas came and left. I don't wanna go back to school, I don't. Dad says that I can take two more days, but dropping out is out of the question.

"Listen," I tell him. "I don't even wanna go to college so what's the point of me graduating? Besides, you need me here now more than ever."

Joe's about to start working full time now at Stanley. He's a family man now. They will stay with us on the farm for a while, Mia and him, but once the baby is born they wanna have their own place.

Once Elliot feels better he will return to San Antonio, I am sure. There's only me to pick up the slack on the farm. Dad says, "Absolutely not. You're going back to school, then off to college."

He just won't listen to me.

"Dad, where's Elliot? I wanna see him," I say.

* * *

Elliot walks to my room and I ask him to close the door and sit by my side. I tell him I'm ready to talk. "I'm ready to tell you everything, but you can't say a word to anyone, promise?"

"But Alex . . . "

"Promise?"

"Promise," he says, smiling.

Elliot holds, then squeezes my hand as I tell him word by word what happened that night. He looks shocked. I didn't spare any details. I can see tears falling out of his eyes. Once I tell him what had happened at the lake, I decide I also wanna tell him about me. I wanna tell him how it all started. I wanna tell him that I wanted to transition. "You know, Elliot . . . you know I have never looked like a girl and I have never felt like one."

"Well, yeah, cause you are our kiddo," he says.

"I am serious about this, Elliot. A boy, that's what I really am."

Elliot looks at me and says, "I don't think I understand you, Alex."

"I'm a boy. I have always felt trapped in this body."

"Alex, I . . . I have no idea what to tell you. I mean, I know you were always different, but . . . what can I say?"

I explain to him that this whole thing is one of the reasons I don't wanna go back to school.

"The farm," I tell him. "All I want is the farm."

Elliot stands up and paces around my room. It's like he's looking for words. He says we are two wounded soldiers. He's right. He also says that, at some point, we both have to go back to the front-lines. "You can't hide. You can't be afraid, Alex. I understand you, believe me. See, part of me wants to just stay here, too, but I know I have to heal and go back. I can't be a farmer. A soldier, that's who I am. I owe it to myself to go back."

I know what he means.

Mia knocks at my door. "Hey guys," she says. She brings me water and my meds. She says George is here, and he's wondering if he can come in. I smile. I like having George around. He's the only one who hasn't asked me a thing.

"Yes, let him in," I say.

Elliot smiles. He kisses my forehead and says, "We'll continue this conversation later, okay?"

"Okay."

George brings movies, magazines, and books. I can tell it's hard for him to see me like this, but he says nothing. Not talking about it makes us both believe nothing happened.

But it did. It did happen. *It* happened to me.

CHAPTER TEN
friends

JAKE'S WAITING FOR ME OUTSIDE. HE'S HOLDING OUR bikes. I have a new one. Dad got it for me after *it* happened.

Jake says, "Ready to ride?"

I tell him, "Yes, but not to school."

We both climb on our bikes and ride all the way to school in silence. As we arrive, we lock our bikes, then Jake says, "It'll all be fine, don't worry. You're not alone. See?" George and Maggie are waiting for us outside school.

"Welcome back," they both say.

The four of us walk in together. I feel everyone's looking at me. We all go to our classrooms.

First period, geometry, Mrs. Lee. This is where it all started. I hesitate to walk in, but Maggie takes me by the arm and says, "You have nothing to worry about. Philip Carson isn't here anymore. His parents sent him to boarding school in Akron, remember?"

I nod.

Mrs. Lee welcomes me back. She tells me I can come once a week with her to work on what I have missed.

When the class starts, Mrs. Smith comes in; she reminds us that this Friday all sophomore students will have a field trip to Cincinnati. "So you can all start seeing your options for college. Please have your parents sign this letter."

I hear some of my classmates excited about the trip. I really don't wanna go, but I guess any place is better than school. I take the letter and put it inside my backpack.

I get my food and as I'm looking for a place to sit down, I see George talking with Jake. They wave to me and tell me they saved me a spot. It seems that they finally became friends, or at least friendly.

Maggie stops at our table for a second to say, "Hi." She asks me how I feel. She caresses my back before she goes to sit with her friends. Jake notices the gesture and once she's gone, he says, "I think Maggie likes you."

I say, "She's been very nice to me, just like you two. It's nice to be friends with her again."

George and Jake exchange looks and then George says, "No, I think Jake is right. Maggie like-likes you. She . . . well, when you decided not to say anything about who hurt you, Maggie went and talked to Mr. and Mrs. Carson."

"Shut up," Jake tells George.

"Well, Alex has the right to know," George replies.

I can't believe what I'm hearing. Maggie? Maggie did that? Jake explains, "She threatened them. She told them she had proof that Philip was the one who attacked you."

I stop eating and push my tray away. I tell them there's no way she has proof; there was no one around.

Jake says, "She told them she had proof, but that doesn't mean she actually did. I think she just wanted to scare them. And it worked. Poof. Philip is out of the picture."

"Now eat this garbage or else you'll never see the end of it. We promised your men we would take care of you," George adds.

"My men?" I ask.

"Yes, your old man and your brothers. Hey, is Elliot single? He is *so* handsome, way more handsome than Joe," George says.

"And *very* straight. You have like zero chance, man," Jake says.

We all laugh. I feel good. Something still hurts inside, but it's good to be back.

* * *

Dad insisted I go on this trip. He was right. Cicny isn't that bad. The road trip has been kinda fun. Maggie sat with me, and George and Jake sat together, and we all talked shit with the rest of our classmates. George started an imitation game, each one of us made the voice and gestures of one of our teachers and the rest had to guess. It was great.

But the best thing is happening now at the university. We were divided into groups, and are taking a campus tour led by college students. This place is fantastic. There are so many buildings and green spaces; it's beautiful. The student union and the library are my favorite places so far.

One of the guides in my group starts talking to me; he seems a bit feminine. His name is Dan. I wonder if he's gay. He's asking me what I plan to study and stuff. I tell him I don't wanna go to college.

"Well, what are you doing here then?"

"Couldn't say no to a field trip."

"Ah. What are your plans then? What do you wanna do when you grow up?"

"My family has a strawberry farm. I plan to be in charge of it."

"Well, then you should study something farm-related," Dan says.

"Farm-related? Whaddya mean?"

"Agriculture, biology, business, maybe even marketing. You should not only own a farm, you should own the *best* farm." He continues, "My dad has cows, my major is agronomy, and I'm studying how to create the best milk in the world, man." Then he winks at me and says, "Besides, girls dig smart boys, eh, Alex? Don't you wanna become one?"

It's happening again, this guy is confusing me for a boy, only this time it doesn't make me happy. I shrug. Then he adds, "You'll love it here. There are people like us—a whole network of support."

"People like us?" I ask.

Dan looks at me, and blushes. "Jesus, that came out wrong," he says.

Dan looks around, as if making sure no one hears us. The rest of the group is ahead of us, so he goes, "I didn't want to offend you or anything . . . it's just . . . Ay, I always do this." He checks again where the rest of the group is. "I'm so sorry. I took for granted you are, you know . . . Maybe I'm wrong. It's just . . . Gee, I'm doing it again," Dan says, covering his face.

"You took for granted I was what?" I ask him.

"Forget it," he says and he invites me to walk with him to join the students.

"Tell me," I say firmly, then add, "Please," to smooth my words.

"You . . . well, I thought you were trans, you know? FTM? Or lesbian—are you lesbian? Oh my God, maybe you ain't any of that and here I am making a fool of myself!"

I can't believe what I'm hearing: what are the chances of meeting someone who sees me this way?

"I guess I, umm . . . I just don't . . . "

"You don't want to talk about it with crazy Dan who you just met?"

"Well . . . "

Dan finds a bench and asks me to sit with him. The rest of the students are taking a break in the garden too.

"I have a friend, a friend like you. He's transitioning, you guys should meet."

"Wow, I've never met anyone . . . you know, like me."

"I remember when I first started. I didn't think I'd fit in. I was scared people wouldn't accept who I was. But it's been better than I hoped. You'll see. Here, why don't we exchange emails."

Unbelievable.

* * *

On our way back to London, everyone is tired, almost everyone is napping. Not me. All I can think about is college. Maybe it's not a bad idea after all? In only a few hours I made a new friend, and, with luck, I can make many more. Friends like me.

CHAPTER ELEVEN
alex the farmer

THE SCHOOL YEAR IS ALMOST OVER. JAKE AND GEORGE say that now that Philip is gone what happened to me will never happen again. I get what they're saying, and I know that Philip will not touch me again, but queer people are bullied all the time. That's what Dan, the guy I met in Cincy, told me. "But that shouldn't stop you from being who you are," he wrote.

We've exchanged some emails and I have also started writing with Jerome, his trans friend. He's shared with me everything about his process. He had an experience like mine, only his was way worse. He was gang raped.

I guess I was lucky that nothing like that happened to me, but what if I'm beat up again? I don't fit in anywhere, and everyone thinks I'm a freak. There are Philip Carsons everywhere.

George keeps pushing me to continue with my transition. For now, I am seeing a therapist and talking about everything that has happened in my life. I understand that transitioning while I'm young is best. But I'm so afraid.

Jake tries to understand me, but he holds onto the idea that I'm a confused girl who likes boy stuff. It's like he doesn't lose faith that one of these days I will fall in love with him and we will live happily ever after. He doesn't say it, but I know that's what's in his heart. He is a hopeless romantic. Just like Maggie.

Maggie has confessed that she likes me, but she is more understanding than Jake. She knows ours is an impossible love. "My mother would never approve," she says with a giggle. I told her I just wanted to be friends; I told her I don't like her like that. I don't know if she believes me.

For now, I just focus on the farm. We're getting everything ready for this year's Strawberry Festival. Mia and I will be in charge of the sales. She doesn't know it, but Joe is going to propose during the Strawberry Ball.

The baby will be born soon. A girl—Mary Alice will be her name; they have already decided. My dad is nervous. He says he can't forget that births and deaths come together in our family. Mia seems relaxed, though. She says, traditions change over time. "This will be a birth and a birth. You'll see, Mr. Jenkins." Mia then looks at me, and adds, "Someone else has to be born too."

Dad says, "A new, better and bigger farm, maybe. I mean, now that Alex has decided to go to college." Dad has stopped threatening to sell the farm. He says we have to make it grow for our growing family.

Oh, Dad. I haven't talked to him. I haven't opened up. I'm not ready. I'm just not ready to be his son. I don't know if he is ready to have me be his son. I don't know if we will ever be ready to face my reality. I don't know if I will dare to let the boy in me be born.

For now I'm just Alex. Alex, the future college student. Alex, the farmer.